"Look, May[be This Isn't] Such A Good Idea,"

Mac whispered. "You're a beautiful woman, and God knows I'm a hungry man, but that's just not enough—not for you."

At first, he thought she hadn't heard him. Her arms were around his neck, and she was clinging to his body, her face burrowed in his throat as she strained against him on tiptoe.

With a low groan, he buried his face in her hair, inhaling the scent of sweet spice and warm woman. "Baby," he murmured, "maybe we'd better quit while we're ahead."

She didn't pretend not to understand him. "Why?" Banner whispered. "You do want me, don't you?"

A ragged laugh escaped him. "Considering the evidence against me, I guess I can't deny it. But, Banner, listen, it's not smart. Not for either of us, honey. You're not cut out for a quick and rough relationship, and I'm not good for anything more than that."

Dear Reader,

When I think of autumn, I think of cool, crisp November nights curled up by the fire...reading a red-hot Silhouette Desire novel. Now, I know not all of you live in cooler climes, but I'm sure you, too, can conjure up visions of long, cozy nights with the hero of your dreams.

Speaking of heroes, Dixie Browning has created a wonderful one in MacCasky Ford, the hero of her *Man of the Month* book, *Not a Marrying Man*. Mac is a man you'll never forget, and he certainly meets his match in Banner Keaton.

November is also a time of homecoming, and Leslie Davis Guccione has been "away from home" for far too long. I know everyone will be glad to see her back with *A Gallant Gentleman*. And if you're looking for something tender, provocative and inspirational, don't miss Ashley Summer's *Heart's Ease*. This story is one I feel very strongly about, and I'd be interested in hearing how you like it.

Rounding out November are a delicious love story from Raye Morgan, *Baby Aboard*, a fiery romp by Carole Buck, *Red-Hot Satin*, and a sexy, spritely tale by Karen Leabo, *Lindy and the Law*.

So, until next month, happy reading!

Lucia Macro
Senior Editor

DIXIE BROWNING

NOT A MARRYING MAN

SILHOUETTE *Desire*®

Published by Silhouette Books New York
America's Publisher of Contemporary Romance

SILHOUETTE BOOKS
300 East 42nd St., New York, N.Y. 10017

NOT A MARRYING MAN

ISBN: 0-373-05678-8

First Silhouette Books printing November 1991

DIXIE BROWNING

has written over forty books for Silhouette since 1980. She is a charter member for the Romance Writers of America, an award-winning author and has toured extensively for Silhouette Books. She also writes historical romances with her sister under the name Bronwyn Williams.

One

In a luxurious hotel suite that had gone unappreciated and largely unused for the past three days, MacCasky Ford poured himself another three fingers of Scotch. He stared at it discontentedly for several moments and then lit a cigarette, his twelfth in the past hour.

Booze, smokes, a king-size bed and a Jacuzzi tub big enough to water a herd of elephants. So what the hell was he waiting for, a brass band?

He'd had that, too. Or the modern equivalent. Maybe that was the trouble. He had all the perks, all the rewards of a job well done, and none of the satisfaction.

The truth was, he'd failed. Five months ago he'd gone after a creep called Julio el Gran, a fugitive who headed a particularly nasty little group of terrorists known as the White Doves. After more than a year and a half undercover he'd finally got them right where he wanted them—

holed up together in a steamy little village near Montana Grande.

But something had gone sour. They'd been tipped. Before Mac could move in for the kill, three State Department employees had been taken hostage, a busload of civilians had been bombed off the road and Mac, who had gone back in after a couple of college kids who fancied themselves photojournalists, had been shot and taken prisoner.

He'd managed to survive, thanks largely to the fact that his body had still been full of antibiotics from another recent "accident." Someone had wired his car, and it had gone off prematurely when he'd switched off a silent alarm from a distance of some ten feet away.

It had been sheer luck—bad for the Doves, good for Mac and his fellow hostages—that a rival group known as *Los Hombres Nieves*, or the Snowmen, had staged a raid on the Doves' sizeable arms cache about two months later. In the excitement Mac had managed to escape and free the other hostages. He'd seen no other survivors.

By the time they made it down from the mountains, the news had reached the valley that the Doves had been firebombed out of existence.

He might even have believed it had someone not sent in a ringer while he was in a hospital in San Felipe. As groggy as he was, he'd been awake enough to see the guy dressed as an orderly shoot a syringe full of something into his IV unit. He'd pretended to rouse, the guy had panicked and fled and Mac had whipped the needle out of his arm. Grabbing only his pants and his shoes, he'd discharged himself out a third-floor window and made his way to a safe house, where he'd put through a call to a certain auto dealer.

Before he'd even boarded the prearranged flight back to the States, a plan had been set into motion. It had been decided that Mac's mission would be declared a success, with Mac taking public credit for wiping out the entire nest of White Doves. Meanwhile, under cover of all the hoopla, two men would quietly take over where Mac had left off, hoping to catch them off guard.

Hoping to stir up more trouble between the two rival groups. Hoping for anything that would enable one or another branch of the service to locate and clean up one more small but virulent cancer on the face of the earth.

Mac stubbed out his cigarette and whispered a gutter expression that had no exact English translation. He'd spent two years in the army and sixteen years of his life in law enforcement. For what? Had he made the world a safer place?

Not noticeably. The players changed, the arenas changed, but the game remained the same. MacCasky had had enough of it. For what seemed a lifetime he'd been hunting down, capturing and delivering to an imperfect, highly fallible justice system some of the most heinous animals on the face of the earth.

Now he wanted out. While most of his body parts were still functioning, he wanted to see if he could build some sort of a life for himself in a part of the world where a knock on the door didn't automatically make him flatten and draw his gun.

Hating every moment of it, he'd gone along with the media blitz, knowing it was necessary if they wanted the remaining Doves off guard long enough to get another couple of men into the area. But all the time he'd been just hanging in until he could escape to Wilkes County, North Carolina, where there was a farm waiting with his name on the deed.

Not much of a farm, to be sure; sixty-odd acres of scrub and rocks, mostly vertical, with a few old buildings and one slow-moving muddy creek where, if he remembered correctly, he could sit all day and fish without having to stir himself to rebait his hook. His grandfather would no longer be there to spin yarns about his trapping-and-moonshining days, but after sixteen years in the field, it still sounded pretty damned fine to MacCasky.

According to the papers, he was a hero. *U.S. Marshal Rescues Embassy Hostages. Drug-Connected Terrorists Killed in Daring Raid.*

So why did he feel like a failure?

Ruthlessly crumpling the tabloid that had covered the story with heavy-handed sensationalism and scant regard for the facts, Mac downed his drink, shuddered and switched on the six-o'clock news. On seeing his own scowling face over the backs of some dozen or so reporters, his head bared to the freezing rain, he switched it off again.

When the hell had he gone gray?

When the hell had he grown old?

Where had his life gone?

"Come on, man, you won't last a month pulling rocking-chair duty. Like I said, I've got this empty office you could move into tomorrow," said Conner Jones. Conner was regional director for the U.S. Marshals. When the two of them had met, Mac had been with the Bureau of Alcohol, Tobacco and Firearms. Shortly after the FBI had relinquished a large chunk of its responsibility over fugitives to the marshals in an effort to conserve manpower, Conner had talked Mac into joining him. But Mac had never even considered moving into administration.

Now he shook his head, grinning. "No way. I've got a farm waiting back in the foothills of North Carolina that I haven't seen in nearly thirty years. You can take your badge and pin it on your—"

"Just asking, ol' buddy. No harm in asking, huh?"

"God, I feel lousy," Mac muttered, flexing his shoulders. He'd caught a chunk of Mercedes in his right deltoid a few years back that still gave him fits in damp weather.

"You know that's the fourth cigarette you've smoked in the past half hour."

"You got a meter on me?"

Conner shrugged. "Too much booze and tobacco can be hazardous to your health, they tell me."

And then both men grinned, both being well aware that there were times when the mere thought of a stiff drink or a cigarette could do more to keep a man slogging against overwhelming odds than all the cholesterol-free health food in the world.

"Know what you need, Mac? A woman."

Lifting a skeptical eyebrow, MacCasky gazed down the considerable length of his own lean, battered carcass. "Yeah, sure. Like I need to go five rounds with Mike Tyson."

"No kidding, d'you ever think of settling down?"

"What the hell do you think I've been telling you? I've got an appointment at Norfolk General at ten in the morning, and then I'm out of here. I plan to spend the foreseeable future mending my roof, one shingle at a time. When and if I finish that job, I might even tackle a few fences. Then again, I might not. Who the hell needs fences?"

"You've got a house, then?" Sipping his Scotch and water, Conner slouched lower in the rose damask chair, a polished Western boot slung across his other knee. Like more than one U.S. marshal since George Washington had pinned on the first star-shaped badge in 1789, he affected a few modest Westernisms in his attire. Conner Jones, at forty, was no family man himself, having been divorced before Mac had ever met him.

"I used to have a house. My granddad's old place. If it's fallen in by now, I'll get a trailer."

"They call it manufactured housing these days. Shows how long you've been out of circulation. Don't take this the wrong way, but I think you ought to look into some type of stress-reduction program before you go back to the real world."

Wordlessly Mac lifted his glass and his cigarette.

"Other than that, I mean. Keep on and you'll be strung up so tight it'll take a battalion of shrinks to untie you."

Mac's boot heels struck the carpeted floor with a dull thud. He scowled at his friend. "In case it escaped your notice, man, I handed in my stress along with my badge."

"Now, that's not necessarily true. Things don't always work like that, MacCasky. You got rid of that chunk of steel in your shoulder, too, but it still gives you the devil, doesn't it?"

"Only when it rains," Mac muttered.

"Yeah, well I got news for you, buddy—the rain ain't going to quit falling just because you hang up your badge. What you need is a course of counseling and maybe a—"

"You know what you can do with your counseling, don't you?"

Ignoring him, Conner kept pushing. "There's this meditation workshop that's supposed to lower your blood pressure by at least—"

"Pin it right next to your badge and sit on it."

"At least let me send you some material."

Mac jumped up, flinched as his knee threatened to give out under him and stubbornly paced the room. "Knock it off, will you? I've got an appointment with Doc Kraemer in the morning. If he dismisses me, that's good enough for me."

"Cap'n Kraemer's a surgeon. I'm talking shrinks."

"Lay off, Con. If I start talking to myself, I'll listen closely, and if it doesn't make sense, I'll come back in, okay?"

The older man looked as if he wanted to argue, but after a moment he grinned. "Yeah. Okay. Look, you got any family around this farm of yours? Cousins, I mean. Maybe a maiden aunt who could cook you a decent meal once or twice a month and haul you back in line if you get too strung out?"

Both men knew that Mac had no immediate family. His background was a matter of record. Parents divorced when Mac was seven, mother remarried, died nine years ago. Father died two years ago.

Mac had been in Lebanon at the time. He'd missed the funeral, but he'd gotten back as soon as he could. It had torn him up to realize that he could have spent a lot more time with the old man than he had. Jackson MacCasky Ford had turned into a bitter, lonely man when his wife had left him. He and the boy had moved around a lot, never settling in any one place for too long.

"No, no cousins, no aunts or uncles, maidens or otherwise," Mac replied, his mind on the half brother he had never bothered to meet.

He'd found the scrapbook after his father's death, when he'd been going through his effects. One of those cheap dime-store things, the pages crumbling around yellowed newspaper clippings. There had been one about Eleanore Ford's marriage to a Virginia businessman named Harrison Keaton—he'd been stunned to learn that his mother had remarried so soon after divorcing Jack Ford.

But that was nothing compared to the bulk of the clippings that had begun with the birth of a son to Eleanore and Harrison Keaton less than a year later. Rory Keaton.

Even now Mac could remember the feelings that had raced through him when he'd learned that he had a half brother, one he'd never even known existed, much less met.

He'd spent the rest of the day poring over the scrapbook, reading about the son of one of Virginia's more prominent citizens, who reportedly excelled in sports, led the debating team at Maury High, won a scholarship to MIT, only to drop out in his second year and enter an all-class sailing race to Saint John's in the Virgin Islands.

Keaton had come in second and flown back in a single-engine plane, buzzing the Wright Brothers Memorial at Kitty Hawk on the way. After that there'd been a series of escapades, which had included stock-car racing, bull fighting and bronc riding at a charity rodeo.

Somewhere along the line he'd gotten married. Mac had forgotten the details. He'd been more interested in this daredevil who seemed hell-bent on defying the odds at every turn. His half brother. Eleanore's son. His only remaining relative.

And then the odds had turned. The last clipping in the book, dated several years later, had been about a skydiving accident that had taken the life of a well-known Virginia sportsman. Rory Keaton had jumped to his death before some ten thousand horrified spectators at a benefit air show.

Shoving away the memories, Mac stood abruptly and continued to pace the plush executive suite, ignoring the pain of his injured knee. Too much introspection gave him heartburn. "Look, do you want another drink or not? I don't mean to rush you, Con, but I've got some calls to make. I ordered myself a new four-by-four yesterday—it ought to be prepped and waiting by now. Soon as I get it registered and tagged and get my driver's license renewed, I need to pick up a few new pairs of jeans and some shirts."

Mac had lost more than twenty pounds over the past few months. He'd always been built more like a workhorse than a thoroughbred. At just under six feet tall, broad of shoulder and narrow of loin, the loss of weight only made him look taller and tougher.

Conner had been gone some twenty minutes when the phone rang. There were three phones in the suite. Mac had come to hate them all. Stubbing out his cigarette, he debated ignoring it. Ten-to-one it would be another reporter wanting to pump him on the hostage situation, the latest political crisis, or the upcoming primaries. It seemed that getting shot up, taken prisoner and generally screwing up before getting himself untangled again had conferred on him some kind of instant expertise in everything from ethnic cuisine to politics.

Lifting the receiver on the seventh ring, he barked into it, "Yeah, okay, okay!"

"Mr. Ford? This is the concierge. There's someone—ah, here to see you," said a tentative-sounding voice.

"Sorry, you must have the wrong room." He hung up.

The phone rang again, and Mac seriously considered shattering an eardrum, but it wasn't the fault of the poor concierge that he'd been hounded by reporters ever since he'd stepped off the helicopter that had flown him down from the debriefing in Washington. That had been the plan, after all.

"All right, all right, look—can you get rid of him for me? There's twenty bucks in it for you if you can get me off the hook."

"But Mr. Ford, I think you'd better—that is, she—"

"She?" Mac's eyes narrowed at that. He'd been accosted by a female from one of the networks this morning who'd damned near followed him into the men's room. "Is she redheaded, about forty or fifty, with a face like the hood ornament on a Mack truck?''

''No, sir, she's more like—well, I'm not sure of her age, but she's small, blond and has sort of greenish eyes . . . I think. She's resting them at the moment.''

Resting them. Resting them?

''You mean she's *sleeping?*''

On a deserted island off the coast of North Carolina, Banner McNair Keaton sat back on her heels and stared at the yellowed newspaper she'd pulled off the top of the stack. Absently she ran a filthy hand over one cheek, leaving behind a trail of grime as she brushed back a wisp of russet hair.

''Hurricane Hugo Batters The Carolina Coast,'' she read aloud. Heavens, that had been . . . how many years ago? That had been the year her great-aunt Pearlie McNair had suffered her first stroke.

Sighing, she placed the paper on top of the discard stack. She was too tired to waste any more time reminiscing. It was nearly dark, and she had tons more stuff to go through. She'd put off the job as long as she could. After taking a year's leave of absence from teaching to look after Aunt Pearlie, and then coming down with a persistent case of flu less than two weeks after her great-aunt had died, she felt an urgent need to wind things up and get back to work.

Or rather, her bank balance felt the urgent need.

True, she could have waited until summer to tackle this business of clearing out umpteen generations of junk and getting the old house ready to turn over to the park service, but Banner had never been one to postpone the inevitable.

She'd spent the past two days saying her goodbyes to the island. There had been a lifetime of memories stored up in the old house, in the creeks and marshes, the scrubby woods and cemeteries. Her favorite was a tiny one—two stones she'd come upon once by accident when she'd gone exploring as a child, marking the graves of two seamen who had died nearly two hundred years before.

There was the creek below Haulover Point, where she'd caught her first fish. Coast Guard Creek, by the old life-saving station. They'd gone out from there the day she'd eaten her first raw oyster. She had watched, fascinated while her father had shucked them, and then cried because he hadn't allowed her to keep the tiny oyster crab for a pet.

Not all the memories had been so sweet. Seven and a half years ago she'd come here to this very house with her brand-new husband. That had been the beginning of her growing up. Another milestone, perhaps, but one she'd prefer to forget.

Rosie, her favorite park ranger, had stopped by just this morning to check on her. Rosie was inclined to worry, but Banner had assured her that she wasn't afraid. There was nothing on the island to fear. She was alone here with no one to bother her.

"Nobody to come to your rescue, either," the young ranger had reminded her. Communications weren't always dependable this time of year, and in the off-season, with manpower cut to the bone, the island wasn't normally patrolled. Rosie had heard through the grapevine that someone was staying on the island and had come up to investigate.

"I'll be careful," Banner had assured her. "I doubt that I'll even leave the house, so you don't have to worry about me. I have enough food, plenty of firewood and plenty of blankets. And if I get bored, I can always reread Aunt Pearlie's old schoolbooks and newspapers."

Even the old man who had brought her across to the island had tried to talk her out of staying. "Weather's like to turn on you, Banner," Captain Julius O'Neal had said. "Look at that sky."

"Not a cloud in it."

"That's what I mean. She's bound to change. I'd worry some if you was to get caught over there by yourself."

"I'd hardly starve, Cap'n Julius. Aunt Pearlie always kept the pantry stocked, and I'm taking over loads of stuff." She was. One box of canned soups and three more of cleaning supplies.

He'd helped her load her parcels on board, disapproval clear on his weathered face, and Banner had tried to reassure him.

"Don't worry, it wouldn't be the first time I got stuck over there in bad weather. Remember that hurricane that took the roof off the net shed? I was alone then, and even the park ranger didn't make it back over for eight days."

Wind had whipped the wool-lined denim coat against the old man's wiry frame as he set a course from Ocracoke to the next island in the Outer Banks chain. "I 'member one skeert youngun eatin' me outta house and home when I finally got back over t' Porchmouth and brung her back across the inlet. You et like you hadn't et in a week!"

Porchmouth. That was what Aunt Pearlie had called the island, too. Most of the older bankers did. "Could I help it if my supplies got rained on and the fish refused to bite?" she asked, watching the familiar landmarks fall behind. She had always loved this ride. She'd always loved the island, but there came a time to say goodbye.

"She was a good woman, Miz Pearlie was. I'll miss 'er."

"I know, Captain Julius," Banner said quietly. "Me, too."

That had been the day before yesterday. Since then, Banner had tackled one room at a time, packing up the few things worth keeping, bagging the rest for disposal. She had cleaned each room as she'd finished, not because the park service required it, but because her aunt would have wanted it done that way. Pearlie McNair had had little money in her life, but more than enough pride to make up for the lack. She had moved to the mainland only when it had become impractical for her to remain alone on the island.

Another full day at the most, Banner figured. Rosie would probably stop by tomorrow, and Banner would ask her to call Captain Julius over on Ocracoke and have him meet her at Haulover Point dock at noon the next day. That would give her a day to finish up the house, and half a day to finish saying goodbye to the island.

Fighting off an unreasonable urge to weep, Banner tackled the shelf of books she'd read as a child—books that she and her mother, her grandmother and her great-aunt had read as children. They were dog-eared, mildewed and infinitely precious, but was there any real point in saving them for another generation of McNairs? Unless she had relatives she'd never heard of, she was the last of the line—a widow with no intention of remarrying. A woman who'd had her chance and lost it.

MacCasky stared at the concierge over the head of the small person standing solemnly beside her, a brown paper bag clutched in her hands. "The hell you say," he repeated disbelievingly for the third time.

The woman in the rose-colored suit with the hotel badge winced. With a warning glance at the child, she said, "Mr. Ford, all I know is that she's been sitting there in the lobby for over two hours, and she had this note pinned to her coat. We thought she was waiting for someone, but...well, after a while, the front desk asked me to check on her."

"And she wanted to see *me?*" Mac stared down at the big-eyed waif, who stared back at him, her pinched features expressionless.

The concierge shrugged. "Your name was on the note. I'm sorry if it inconveniences you, sir, but you can hardly expect the hotel to take responsibility. The letter is addressed to a MacCasky Ford, so I brought her to you. My responsibility ends there. Are you sure you don't know who she is? A relative? The child of a business associate, perhaps, who'll be along later to collect her?"

She stopped short of asking if she could be the child of a woman friend, but the implication was there.

Mac scowled, something he'd been doing almost constantly lately, it seemed. "I don't have a relative, I don't have a business associate, and as for the rest of what you're thinking, you're way off base."

"I assure you, sir, I wasn't thinking—"

"Right!"

The child squirmed, shifting her negligible weight from one leg to the other. She seemed to bend over just a bit, but in the skimpy red velvet coat, with a paper sack held against her, it was hard to be sure.

She sighed. It was the first sound either of the adults had heard from her, and they both stared down at her, at a loss as to how to handle the situation. MacCasky didn't know the kid. Children in general were an alien species as far as he was concerned. The hotel employee seemed almost as uncomfortable as he was.

Did she think he was lying? Did she think, for God's sake, that the kid was one of his by-blows? He might not be the world's smartest man, but at least he'd taken care not to leave behind any unwanted reminders of his infrequent affairs.

If some broad was claiming otherwise, she'd have the devil of a time proving it, that was all he had to say.

"Well . . . call housekeeping if you need anything else," the concierge murmured, easing toward the elevators.

"Hey, look, you can't just drop off a kid and leave her with a strange man! You don't know me from Adam. For all you know, I might be the worst kind of creep."

"Oh, Mr. MacCasky, everybody in the hotel—everybody in the country knows who you are. You're kin to the Keatons that own Keaton Plaza over on the boulevard. You're a hero. You risked your life to save those poor people over in—"

MacCasky's response was short, to the point and extremely crude. The woman gasped. The child showed no response at all.

"Look, just read the letter, why don't you?" The concierge returned, unpinned the note, placed it in his unresisting hand and then stepped back into the elevator. "I'm sure it'll explain everything."

If there was an explanation for something so bizarre, Mac seriously doubted that he'd find it in the small pink envelope pinned to the kid's chest. "Hey, wait! Look, I'm supposed to meet a car dealer in twenty minutes! What the hell am I supposed to do with her?"

The concierge shrugged. Just as the elevator doors closed, she said, "I think she might have to go to the bathroom."

Mac stood in the doorway, a pale, stern-looking man dressed in new jeans, a new navy flannel shirt and ancient Western boots. In his hand was a pink envelope. On his haggard face was an expression comprised of one part fury and two parts bafflement.

The small person stared up at him. To his knowledge, she hadn't spoken a word since she'd shown up at the hotel. Maybe she wasn't old enough to talk. How old did a kid have to be? She was about three feet long—he tried and failed to translate that into years.

"How old are you, anyway, kid?"

Gravely she held up a tiny hand, four fingers extended and a thumb that wavered in and out, finally settling on out.

"Five, huh?"

Silence. She continued to stare up at him with those enormous cloudy green eyes, as if she knew a hell of a lot more than she was willing to divulge for reasons that he could only guess at.

It wasn't an auspicious start to his retirement. "Can you talk?"

If eyes could be said to speak, hers were saying plenty, none of it what he wanted to hear. Why did he keep reading pain, loneliness and fear into her silences? He was no damned gypsy fortune-teller!

Unwilling to close the door, taking her into his suite, Mac braced his shoulders against the door frame and ripped open the envelope, trying to ignore her pinched little face staring up at him. He wasn't taking any chances on getting himself set up, not until he knew what the hell kind of game was being played out here. He hadn't survived this long by taking chances.

Before he read the first word, his mind had automatically catalogued a large amount of information. The letter itself was brief, written in a childish hand. Rounded letters with an uneven slope, circle-dotted *i*'s, fancy capitals with a flourish under his name. As for the stationery, it was inexpensive, the kind that could be bought in most variety stores.

But it was neither the stationery nor the penmanship that brought him up ramrod straight where he stood. It was the message.

I saw you on the television news, and it said you were Rory's half brother. Her name is Tiffany Eleanore Keaton. She's Rory's daughter, but now I'm giving her to you. She's no trouble to look after. I'm getting married, and he doesn't want her, so don't try to find me because I'm leaving the country.

There was no signature.

"Oh, no," he whispered. Then, "Oh, no—hell, no! No way, kid." Not now, not when he had his whole life all mapped out—not when he had finally reached the place where he could bow out and let someone else take over the world's problems. "Sorry, honey, but it just won't wash. You and me, we're going to catch your mama before she gets too far away and remind her of a few obligations, right? You don't want to be stuck with an old crock like me, now do you?"

For the first time since he'd started to read the note, Mac glanced down at the small figure beside him, and then wished he hadn't. She was no longer looking at him, she was staring at the floor. From where he stood, he could see a tear begin to trace a wet path down her cheek.

And that wasn't the only thing that was wet. Even as he stared, the carpet slowly darkened between her feet.

Swallowing a lump the size of Mount Mitchell in his throat, he knelt and awkwardly touched her on the shoulder. "Hey—kid, I'm sorry. You should have said something."

When there was no response—at least none except for a strangled sob, he lifted her up from under her arms, holding her away from his body, and carried her through to his palatial bathroom. "Can you handle it from here, hmm? Just throw your wet skivvies in the tub. I'll send for a maid to come help you mop up."

She didn't move from where he'd set her down. She was still hanging on to that battered paper sack as if it were a life raft, and Mac couldn't quite bring himself to shut the door on her. She looked so damned little! Like a small wet mouse in a marble palace. "Come on now, sport—you just skin on out of those wet whatchamacallits now, you hear? Wouldn't want you to catch cold, would we?"

He backed out, revolted at the note of false cheerfulness in his voice. He'd never uttered such inanities in his life—what had got into him?

The question was not what had got into him, but what he was going to do about it! Because one thing was for damned sure—he wasn't going to be the patsy just because his late half brother's widow felt like shedding a few responsibilities. No way!

Grabbing up the nearest phone, he began dialing. Housekeeping first. "Look, I've got a kid up here—she's a girl, about three, three-and-a-half feet tall. Hell, I don't know—five, I think! Anyhow, she's my niece, and the thing is, she's ah—wet herself, and I'm not about to— look, I'll make it worth your while, okay? Just get on up here!"

Next he buzzed the concierge. "This is Mac Ford. Did anyone see how the kid got here? I seriously doubt if she caught a cab by herself, don't you?"

He listened for less than a minute, his expression growing more and more thunderous. "What the hell do you mean, a hired delivery service, you guess? Didn't you *see?*" And then, "Can people do that? Hire people to deliver kids?"

And then, "Dammit, this is no time for wisecracks, woman, I'm in trouble here! The kid's supposed to be my niece, but I don't know anything about taking care of babies—besides, I'm leaving town in the morning—all right, all right, but I'm not finished with you!"

Next he called the auto dealer to tell him he was running late, and asked if he could have his new vehicle delivered to the hotel.

There was that damned physical tomorrow, too. For two cents he'd cancel his appointment, but he had a feeling they'd track him down.

The last call he placed was to Conner Jones. And then he dealt out gratuities to the maid and housekeeper who had mopped up, dried off and outfitted his niece. An extra ten went to the maid who'd discovered that her patent leather shoes were a full size too small and most of the things in her bag were outgrown, as well.

He'd sent her shopping, and she'd come back two hours later laden with packages. By that time the kid had been asleep on the cot he'd had brought in, clutching a dirty sock that had been stuffed and made into a monkey with a clown's hat. She'd woken up, tried on her new clothes at the maid's insistence while Mac ordered a meal sent up to the suite.

Then she'd put away enough food to satisfy two normal adults and thrown up all over his bed.

Mac slept on the love seat. He'd spent worse nights. But not much worse.

Early the next morning he checked in with Conner Jones, only to be told that no delivery service on record had made a delivery of a child anywhere, and none had delivered anything to that particular hotel.

Grimly silent, Mac bundled an equally silent Tiffany Eleanore Keaton, resplendent in new jeans, new shoes and a new down-filled coat and hood, into his brand-new Blazer four-by-four and headed for Norfolk General.

He'd struck out on the delivery service, but the wheels were in motion now. He'd know something by the time he got done with his physical. If Mrs. Rory Keaton, widow of the late Rory Keaton, thought she could elude the service that had tracked down fugitive spies, turncoats, drug lords and one of the most infamous Nazi war criminals of all time, she was in for a small surprise.

Two

It was impossible to talk over the drone of the open boat. Mac would have much preferred to stand at the console with the old man he'd hired to run them across to Portsmouth Island, but he could hardly leave the kid on her own. She looked lost enough, as it was. And scared.

And dammit, she still hadn't opened that pinched-up little mouth of hers except to stuff down everything he'd had sent up from the kitchen. Bolting ice cream was one thing—bolting fried chicken was another. He'd had to force her to slow down and chew her food, because he wasn't sure he'd have the nerve to do the Heimlich maneuver on anything that small.

It was nothing less than criminal. People who didn't want kids should take steps to see that they never had any. Even now, after two days, he felt like hitting something when he thought about the report Conner's man had sent in.

She hadn't been that hard to trace. Banner Keaton currently lived in a small town in northeast North Carolina. She was some kind of an artist, which could mean just about anything. After teaching at a junior college for a few years, she'd dropped out and moved out of town. The college had said simply that she was on a leave of absence. If they had a forwarding address, the girl he'd talked to wasn't handing it over, not without a warrant, and Mac wanted to keep this unofficial as long as he could, for the kid's sake. The people in the Keaton woman's apartment building had been curious, but not overly forthcoming. Mrs. Keaton kept to herself, they said. Pleasant, but reserved. Not one to get involved.

As for the kid, no one seemed to know anything at all about her. There were a lot of children in the neighborhood, they said. One more or less probably wouldn't even be noticed. It had been the apartment super who had come through for him. The Keaton woman had needed cartons to take to some cottage or other on the Outer Banks—a place called Portsmouth Island. The super happened to have a stack of banana boxes a new tenant had put out on the curb, and as they were sturdy and easy to handle, she'd loaded them into her station wagon and headed east on Highway 168.

Shooting a puzzled glance at the slight, silent figure beside him, Mac tried to put it all together. Now that he'd tracked her down, he wasn't at all certain he should just hand over the kid and leave. If the woman had dumped her once, she'd do it again. Next time she might not bother to hunt up a relative.

He couldn't trust her. Which meant he was going to have to find some way to keep tabs on her. And that was going to be a pain. If there was one thing he didn't need at this stage of his life, it was entanglements. The service had been all the entanglement any man needed, and now that he was

free of it, he'd sworn to live the rest of his life on his own
terms and his own turf!

Mac stared out across the glassy, dark green water and
swore silently. Whether the kid was actually his kin or not,
it made him physically ill to think of anything so small and
helpless being put in such jeopardy. He'd seen enough
children wasted to last a hundred lifetimes.

The boat swerved around a channel marker, and the
tiny, huddled figure beside him leaned against his arm and
then quickly righted herself. Glancing down, he could see
that she was gripping the edge of the seat, her tiny knuckles blue-white.

Damn. He should have got her a pair of gloves. He'd
picked up half a dozen more pairs of underpants and a
couple more pairs of jeans, just in case, but he hadn't even
thought about gloves.

"Hey, honey—you okay down there?" he said in a soft
rumble that was meant to be reassuring.

She nodded her head in a quick jerky movement. A wisp
of white-blond hair slipped out from underneath her hood,
and Mac resisted the shocking urge to tuck it back inside.

He hadn't touched her any more than necessary. Not
that he had anything against kids—he just wasn't used to
them. They made him nervous. Big-eyed little girls with
pointy little chins and pinched-up little mouths who didn't
utter a sound, even when they cried, made him kind of
crazy.

"Look, it's going to be all right," he said gruffly. "We
found your mama—she's waiting for you right now."

Waiting, but with God knows who. Some creep who
wants to cash in on Keaton's life insurance, no doubt. And
because he felt guilty at the thought of returning her to
someone who had dumped her out like a sack of garbage,
he made a rash promise. "What d'you think—I say she's

probably got a big, sizzling steak and a pan full of fries on the stove right this minute... how's that sound, huh?''

He was desperate. Maybe the thought of a meal would get a reaction out of her. Nothing else had. He'd never seen such a quiet kid—nor had he ever seen one go through so many groceries. You'd think she hadn't eaten in a week.

It took close to forty-five minutes to reach the island. The distance hadn't looked that great when he'd checked it out on a map the night before, but it had taken four and a half hours just to get to the boat dock.

Engine at a slow idle, the old man eased the boat alongside a sturdy pier and slung a line around one of the pilings. "How long ye think ye'll be?" he asked as Mac lifted the child up out of the boat and leapt up after her, both her bag and his shaving kit tucked under his arm.

"I dunno, long enough to deliver the kid. How far did you say it was to Mrs. Keaton's place?"

"That'd be the old McNair place. 'Bout a mile, mile and a half. Foller this 'ere road to the first graveyard, turn left, take a right after ye cross over the creek, and then another right when ye come to three tombstones settin' off to theyselves. Can't miss it."

Graveyards, creeks and tombstones. If a woman wanted to disappear, and the Keaton woman obviously did, then she'd picked the right place to do it. He'd learned that the island was owned by the park service and was largely deserted this time of year except for the occasional birdwatcher.

"Look, give me a couple of hours, can you do that?"

The old man studied him intently for a moment, and then scanned the sky. The sun was still shining, but a milky haze was beginning to form out over the ocean. "Well now, maybe I can and maybe I can't. Make it a hour and a half. If ye're not on the end of the pier by then, I'll c'lect ye when I come to fetch Miz Keaton, that suit ye awright?"

After a moment's deliberation, Mac nodded. He was ninety-nine percent sure the woman was here. Captain Julius had said he'd brought her over. Alone. But that didn't mean someone else hadn't met her here and taken her off the island some other way. She'd said she was getting married. She'd also said she was leaving the country—and from what he'd seen so far, she damned near had!

For a woman who was supposed to be dropping out of sight, she hadn't made any effort to cover her trail so far. Maybe this was only her starting point. He had a feeling his work was just beginning.

"Hour and a half, then," Mac agreed. "Probably won't take that long." He set out with a long-legged stride as the boat veered away from the pier. Halfway down the dock he glanced over his shoulder and frowned. "Hey, step on it, half-pint—we've got a long ways to go and a short time to get there, as the song says. You wouldn't want your supper to get cold, would you?"

She started walking then, but it was easy to see that he'd never make it in time if he had to slow his pace to suit hers. "Come here, Uncle Mac'll give you a lift, huh? Hoist that little nose of yours up here where you can get a whiff of the wind—is that steak I smell, or am I dreaming?"

He almost thought she was going to smile, but she didn't quite make it. She did, however, allow him to lift her up onto his shoulder. Not that she cooperated, but she didn't actually resist.

Were all kids this way? It was a wonder any of them survived! How the hell did you know how to treat them if they wouldn't even tell you when they were hungry, or when they had to go to the bathroom?

"Hey—" He stopped suddenly on the narrow footpath that wound through the marsh towards the distant woods. "You don't, do you? Have to go to the john, I mean?"

He'd sent her into the ladies' room at the ferry stop on
Ocracoke Island, but around all this water...

"Look, you can tell me, honey. I'll wait. I'll turn my
back and watch those pelicans flying out over the sound
until you give me the all clear, okay?" And when she didn't
reply, he repeated, "Okay, half-pint? Tiffany? Eleanore?"

*She'd been named for his own mother. His mother—
Rory's mother—had been this little kid's grandmother.*

Jesus. He didn't need this.

"Okay, off we go, but if you get to feeling, uh, uncomfortable, just kick me in the ribs or something, will you? I
don't think either one of us would appreciate being wet
down with the wind picking up the way it is."

Banner scribbled "save" on another box and jammed
the pencil back through the heavy coil of hair on top of her
head. At this rate she was going to have to rent a ferry to
move her out of here. Who would have thought there
would be this much to keep in a summer place that had
been used so little for the past several years?

A bittersweet smile touched her pale face and faded just
as quickly. Rory had loved the idea of owning his own
private island. Even after she'd explained that the park
service actually owned the island, but that her family had
a lifetime right to Gideon's Retreat, as some ancestor had
named the gaunt, unpainted frame house, he had considered it his private island. He'd been full of impossible
plans—boat basins, a runabout, guest cottages—maybe
even a small landing strip.

She'd tried to explain that the park service wouldn't
permit any building of cottages or landing strips, even if
Aunt Pearlie would agree. Nor would the Corps of Engi-
neers permit the dredging of a yacht basin, but as usual,
Rory heard only what he wanted to hear.

All that had begun to change soon after they'd arrived. Banner didn't know what Rory had been expecting when he'd insisted they honeymoon here at the cottage, but she would never forget his face when he'd got his first look at the bleak old cottage with its Gothic gables and leaking roof.

She'd been barely twenty-one then—starry-eyed, naive and wildly impressionable. Rory Keaton, in town for a balloon rally, had swept across her small-town horizon like a blazing comet, and within a week she'd married the handsome, wealthy young playboy.

He'd claimed to love what he called her serenity. Before the honeymoon was even over, her "serenity" had begun to lose its appeal.

He'd called her provincial. Boring. Inhibited.

They'd spent a day and a half on the island, while Rory alternately made love to her and criticized the mildewed bedding, the rust-stained water, the primitive plumbing and her for not telling him the place was a dump.

Banner had tried to warn him that Gideon's Retreat was hardly an imposing dower unless one happened to be in love with the Outer Banks. But, as she soon came to realize, Rory lived in a glamorous, adventurous world of his own creation.

They'd closed down the cottage, caught a ride back to Ocracoke and ended up flying down to Florida, where Banner had sat in her hotel room while Rory competed in a marlin tournament. On the way home they'd stopped off in North Wilkesboro, where she'd watched in horrified fascination as her brand-new husband had roared around a motor speedway at sickening speeds with a stock-car racing pal.

The marriage had lasted eighteen months. It had been a true attraction of opposites in the beginning—her diffidence versus his daredevil ways. Within a year the serenity he had claimed to admire was a thing of the past. Rory's thirst for conquest had not stopped at fishing tournaments or stock-car races, stunt flying or mountain climbing. He'd gone through two full-blown affairs and any number of flings, as she was later to discover.

It had been her pregnancy that had brought things to a head. Rory had wanted her to get rid of it. He'd insisted, in fact. It was bad enough being tied down by a wife—he wasn't about to be strangled by a family, as well. Forced to choose between her husband and child, Banner had chosen her baby. Four months after Rory had filed for a divorce, she had lost her little girl, as well.

Now she stared out over the marsh, oblivious to the distinctive silhouette of the old abandoned lifesaving station, oblivious to the increasingly threatening sky. Raking grimy fingers through her hair, she shoved her topknot several degrees off center and tried to remember whether or not she'd eaten lunch. Or even breakfast.

After three days of nothing but canned soup, she was almost ready to gamble on one of the labelless, rusted cans in the pantry. What she wouldn't give now for a double cheeseburger with bacon and tomato and a large root beer.

What she wouldn't give now for a hot shower! She'd never felt, and probably never looked, so filthy in her entire life. That, from a painter and a compulsive gardener, was saying a lot.

So far today she'd added to the pile one more box of stuff to be burned, one to be disposed of and two to be saved—goodness knows why. There was one more room to go. The kitchen. Maybe she'd bequeath all those rusty cans of corned beef hash, hominy grits and creesy greens to the National Park Service. Who knows, Rosie the ranger might find herself stranded over here someday and prefer gambling to starving to death.

And speaking of Rosie, it was about time for her to show up. The park ranger had promised to try to get back over sometime today, knowing that Banner was here alone.

As if on command, footsteps crossed the wooden front porch and someone knocked on the screen. Banner jumped up off the floor, blinked rapidly as spots swam before her eyes and then hurried to the front of the house. Goodness, she was going to have to eat something, quick! "Coming, Rosie, don't bruise your knuckles," she called out.

The ranger sounded as if she were in a hurry. Or maybe the winter mosquitoes were getting to her.

MacCasky was almost certain she was in there. There was no smoke coming from the chimney at the moment, but the fresh smell of it hung heavy in the air. If she'd flown, it had been within the hour. She couldn't have gotten far, unless she'd been picked up by a chopper, and he'd have heard that, even out in the inlet. Sound carried over water, and he had a good ear for choppers.

According to the map he'd picked up, there were three logical places for a boat to come in. The one he'd used was the most likely, but not necessarily the one she'd use if she didn't want to be observed.

"It's okay, kid, we'll find her." Was it his imagination, or did those small arms actually tighten about his neck? She curled her icy fingers into the sheepskin lining of his leather coat, making him wish he'd bought one just like it for her. The coat the maid had bought for her would have to do for now.

He had just lifted his hand to knock again when the door opened. Mac pushed one booted foot inside before she could slam it shut again. "Mrs. Keaton, I've brought you your daughter. Thanks for the offer, but I'm afraid I've made other plans."

Before she could open her mouth, he had sized her up, using skills long since honed to a fine edge. She wasn't at all what he'd expected, and as a result, he was watching her carefully for a reaction to his statement.

And then his flinty gray eyes widened as he watched the wisp of a woman before him crumple to the floor without a sound.

After a lot of years as a marshal, and a few years before that with the Bureau of Alcohol, Tobacco and Firearms, MacCasky had come to expect the unexpected. Dealing with it was his specialty.

This time he damned near lost it. Carefully lowering the child to the gritty porch floor, he said, "Stay put, half-pint. Your mama seems surprised to see us."

Surprised? He'd had less than thirty seconds to interpret the expression on her face. Life-or-death decisions often took less time than that. But if there'd been fear or guilt mixed in with the surprise, he'd missed it. His initial reaction had been that she wasn't at all what he'd been expecting. Before he'd had time to digest even that thought, she was collapsing.

Mentally filing and cross-referencing facts, Mac knelt beside the woman's crumpled form. She seemed intact— nothing broken. No sharp edges to strike as she went down. Age? Probably around thirty. She looked younger except for the eyes. They'd looked older. Sad. The word flashed through his mind, but he dismissed it as inexact and irrelevant. Five feet five, a hundred and eight or thereabouts. Middle European extraction, with a dash of Latina somewhere in the distant past.

"Ma'am? Lady, let's get out of the door so we can close it, all right? Look, I'm going to lift you up and take you inside now. Don't be frightened, I'm not going to hurt you or anything." If he hadn't just hung up his badge, he could have used it to reassure her.

Reassure her! What the hell was he doing trying to re-assure a woman who would dump her kid on a stranger and run out? By rights, he ought to take her in and turn her over to the authorities and let them sort this mess out!

She was even smaller than he'd thought. Under a pair of khakis and a couple of shirts, all several sizes too large, she was nothing. Bird bones. No color at all in her face—even her lips were pale.

But not her hair. There was nothing pale about that. Even in the somber light of this stark and barren room, her hair took on a life of its own. Technically it would be classed as medium brown, but that was just because they didn't have a category for hair like this. Long, thick, the color of iron rust on a cloudy day, it glowed against her ivory skin like banked coals.

Carefully he lowered her onto a piece of furniture that might have been designed by the Marquis de Sade. Like the other pieces in the grim, white-painted room, it was made of black oak, covered in faded black leather that had passed its prime at least a half of a century ago. If there'd ever been any padding under those slabs, it had long since petrified.

But it was the best he could do. "Close the door, will you, honey? Then come stand here by your mama while I go see if I can find a wet cloth or something."

She was beginning to stir. "No—I'm all right."

"You sure? Whoa—don't try to get up, just tell me where everything is and I'll get you some brandy." At the look on her face, he retrenched. "Whiskey?" And then, "Okay, then, you name your poison. You need something to jump start you—come to think of it, I could use something myself."

Her eyes had never left his face, and for reasons that escaped him completely, Mac found himself trying to soften his normally harsh expression. He was not a man given to softness. Or to small talk. Nor did she warrant his consideration. But there was the kid to think of. This was her mother. "Uh—I hope you don't mind, but I sort of promised the half-pint here a steak and fries for supper."

His lips twisted into a grimace of a smile, and that seemed to fascinate the woman, because she stared at his mouth until he turned toward the child. "Come here, honey, say hello to your mama—she's not feeling so hot." And to the woman, he said in an undertone, "I don't know what kind of game you're playing, lady, but I'm not a part of it, and neither is this little girl. Either we straighten this business out right here, or I'm taking you in on a charge of child abandonment."

Skin that had been pale before lost the last vestige of color. She looked as if she were on her last legs and sinking fast.

And then it hit him. "Oh, Jesus," he muttered, unconsciously gathering the child against his side with one arm while he knelt beside the woman on the mission oak couch. "You're sick, aren't you? But why the hell didn't you—" He turned to the child and said, "Honey, why don't you go see if you can locate the bathroom. I'll bet you could use one about now, couldn't you? Then come back and tell me where the kitchen is, and I'll see what I can round up to eat."

Dutifully and without uttering a sound, Tiffany Eleanore Keaton turned and left the room. Mac listened until the sound of her small sneakers disappeared down the bare-floored hallway, and then he turned back to Keaton's widow. "Okay, you're going to level with me while she's out of here. I don't want her upset any more than she already is. One thing first—can she talk? Does she ever talk, I mean?"

A branch scraped against the side of the house, and Mac ignored it. Just as he ignored the darkening sky and the increasing moan of the wind. "Lady, if you're sick, then I'll do what I can to see that you get help, but no more lying, right? And no more neglecting that little girl in there."

"Who *are* you? What do you want with me?"

He wasn't prepared for the quality of her voice. It was deep for a woman, and soft. *Husky* would be the best word to describe it. Somehow it went with her looks, but it definitely didn't go with the impression he'd formed from that childishly scrawled note.

And then he forgot the voice and thought about the words. "What do you mean, who am I? You know damned well who I am. If you don't, and you turned your child over to me anyway, then lady, you're in one bunch of trouble!"

They glared at each other for an immeasurable period of time. At least MacCasky glared. The Keaton woman looked...

He couldn't put his finger on how it was that she looked. If he'd been expecting panic, it wasn't there. Nor was guilt. Nor were any of the other emotions he would normally have expected from a woman who had tried to palm off her child on an unsuspecting stranger.

Mac swore, and the woman swung a leg off the couch at the same time a kind of high-pitched rasp sounded through the house.

"Oh, darn, I should have warned her," she whispered. "I forgot to fill the tank after the last flush. We don't have power, you know. The generator's been out of gas for years. It's pitcher pumps and buckets."

She sat up and Mac backed off. There was something decidedly screwy here, and until he figured it out, he wasn't about to go off and leave that little girl on her own. Either this woman wasn't playing with a full deck, or she was one hell of an actress. Either way, he was going to hang around for a while. Tomorrow would be soon enough to get back to civilization. The farm had waited thirty years—it would wait another few days.

"Do you think you could manage a cup of coffee?" He slid a hand inside his bulky leather coat and felt for his cigarettes. He was long overdue a smoke.

And then he thought better of it. If the woman was sick—in the body, that was, and not just the head—then maybe he'd better hold off until he could step outside. And he wasn't about to do that until he knew for sure the kid would be all right. Hell, even he had heard the story of Hansel and Gretel. And while the woman didn't exactly look like a witch—more like a sleeping princess, in fact— a man couldn't be too careful.

As it turned out, it was tea bags or nothing. Grudgingly Mac took two, soaked them in boiling water until it turned black and then scalded his tongue. He'd never developed a taste for tannic acid, but in an emergency he could adapt.

The Keaton woman was standing at the propane range, stirring canned milk, honey and cocoa powder. It looked good to him—which was a measure of how far a man could sink in a few short hours.

"You warm enough now, honey? Want to take your coat off? Show Mama your new duds, why don't you?" His eyes were accusing as he stared at the slender back that seemed to stiffen every time he spoke to or about the child. In a falsely casual tone, he said, "For some reason everything she had with her was at least two sizes too small. The housekeeper said her little toes were all bent under—"

"Would you *stop* that?" The woman spun around, a dripping spoon held tightly in her hand. "If this is some elaborate practical joke, then it's gone far enough! Who put you up to it? Rory's father? He was always a hard man, but to my knowledge he was never actually cruel."

"Whoa, back up a minute here. Are you trying to claim—" Mac glanced at the child, who sat on the other side of the kitchen table, her large green eyes trained on the pot on the stove. He'd fed her two hot dogs and a big soft drink on the way down from Norfolk, and a couple of candy bars on the Ocracoke ferry, but she was obviously hungry again.

The wind moaned under the broken gingerbread trim on the eaves, and Mac saw Tiffany's eyes shift warily to the window. It wasn't quite five o'clock, but already it was getting dark outside. "It's only wind, honey. Maybe it smells that hot chocolate your mama's boiling up and wants to come inside and have some, right?" He smiled, but evidently he wasn't all that convincing. What did he know about talking to kids?

The Keaton woman stared at him for a moment, sent another wary look at the window and then turned her attention back to the stove.

"Look, we'll talk later," Mac said tersely, addressing the woman. "Right now I'd like to see this little girl put away a steak and a side order of fries, and top it off with a slab of chocolate cake. She's had a long day."

Suspiciously he watched her every move. Watched while her rust-stained hair slipped down onto the back of her neck. Watched her eyes—too large and too dark for such a small, pale face—move from the kid to him and back again.

And then she smiled. At the kid—not at him. For the first time it occurred to Mac that he just might be in more trouble than he'd ever found in Lebanon, Bangkok, Medellín or Montana Grande.

Three

There was no refrigeration. There was no place on the island to buy groceries or anything else. As far as Mac-Casky could determine, there wasn't a living soul closer than Ocracoke, on the other side of a broad, turbulent inlet. Outside, the wind howled like a pack of tomcats, and now and then a burst of rain raked the side of the old house, rattling the tall, naked windows.

"Why don't you go lie down, Mrs. Keaton? I can heat up something for short stuff here. You'd settle for a few cans of soup, wouldn't you, honey?"

It was the child he addressed, but it was the woman who answered. "There's tomato," she said. "My mother used to add a little bit of canned milk and a spoonful of sugar. Do you like it that way, darling?"

Mac's irregular features hardened as he braced both fists on the table and leaned over a scarred kitchen chair that revealed some half a dozen coats of different-colored paint. His angular jaw, in need of a shave, thrust aggressively. "I *said* I'd do it. Don't put yourself out on our account, lady, because I'm not impressed."

Her eyes were the color of fine molasses—dark in the center, paler, almost greenish, where the light struck them. The kind of eyes that could seep into a man's soul if he didn't watch out. Damned if she wasn't making *him* feel guilty.

Mentally he chalked up one more mark against her.

"There's probably a can of corned beef hash in the pantry," she said, ignoring both his rudeness and his scowl. "If you're not afraid of a little rust on the outside of the can, I can heat it for you." In contrast to the wildness outside the house, her voice sounded too controlled, too quiet.

Things weren't going according to plan. Not according to *his* plan, at any rate. Something felt decidedly screwy here, and Mac had learned a long time ago that when things didn't feel right, it was time to start figuring out which way to jump.

The look he gave her didn't cut her any slack. "Soup for the kid, nothing for me. We'll talk after she's taken care of." It was a threat, not a promise.

Through narrowed eyes, he watched her work. She had a way of moving that would have won the approval of any efficiency expert, accomplishing her ends with a minimum of motion. Watching her move quietly about the bleak old kitchen, he began to relax. After a few minutes he even forgot to scowl.

She was still too pale. There was a streak of dirt on her cheek, but no hint of makeup. There was something almost childlike about her mouth—about its softness, its bruised-rose-petal color. But the effect it was having on him was decidedly *un*childlike.

His own lips tightened unconsciously. Okay, so she was pale. She could have been lying when she'd said she wasn't sick—that she'd just skipped a couple of meals and then jumped up too fast. It would explain a whole lot. If she'd just discovered that she had some sort of debilitating or even terminal illness, it would explain her dropping at his feet that way. God, even now he broke out in a cold sweat thinking about it! It would also explain why she had been so eager to hand over the kid to someone else.

But why him? Why not the old man? From all reports, Harrison Keaton could well afford to take on another mouth to feed. An army of 'em. He'd probably insist on it, seeing that the kid was his only link to posterity.

Shifting the various pieces of the puzzle in his mind, Mac searched for a perfect fit as he continued to watch his late half brother's widow. With one hand she took a dull, hand-cranked can opener out of a drawer; with the other, she reached for a can. A step here, a turn there, bend from the waist to slide a pot out from under the counter, reach up to take a mug down off an overhead shelf.

It was like a ballet. Mac had seen his first one of those some ten years before, when he'd briefly cultivated a French dancer. The manager of the troupe, who had escaped before he could be brought to trial, had been ferrying top secret documents back and forth between countries, hidden among trunks full of tights, toe shoes and tutus. For nearly three years they'd been after the little weasel while he evaded some of the best men in the service.

"Shall I fry the hash, too, or are you afraid to take a chance?"

Mac's attention snapped back to the present. That was why he couldn't take his eyes off her, he told himself—not because she was any great beauty, but because she reminded him of whatshername, the ballet dancer. Same willowy strength, same doe-eyed expression.

Only the Keaton woman's doe eyes were real, not painted on. Her pallor came not from stage makeup, but from nature. Or illness.

"Is that your real hair color?"

She froze over like a winter pond. "Whether it is or not is no business of yours, Mr..."

"Mac Ford."

"And if you're still holding out for steak and french fries, I'm afraid you're in for a disappointment, Mr. McFord. I wasn't expecting guests." She gave him a frigid look and turned away to take down a bowl.

"Ford will do. That's Mac as in MacCasky. And I'd hardly call your daughter a guest, Mrs. Keaton." He could deliver a hell of a lot more ice than she could, if it came to a contest.

"Mr. Ford, while you and your small friend are more than welcome to share anything I have here, I wish you would stop referring to her as my daughter." Banner looked beseechingly at the child. "I'd love to have a little girl just like you, darling, but I'm afraid wishing won't make it true, will it? Did you tell Mr. Ford I was your mother? Is it a game?"

Mac's voice, when he answered for the child, was dangerously quiet. "No, Mrs. Keaton—you are Mrs. Keaton, aren't you? Mrs. Rory Keaton? Widow of the late—"

"I'm Banner Keaton, yes."

"Banner Keaton," he repeated, frowning. Sliding two fingers into his right hip pocket, he withdrew a crumpled pink envelope and tossed it onto the table. "Then I guess you recognize this."

Even as he spoke the words, Mac knew the answer. Facts could lie—his instinct seldom did. He watched silently as she picked up the envelope and studied it, making no effort to open it. Her hands were small and well shaped, the fingernails short, unpolished. Firm hands rather than soft ones, he'd be willing to bet.

Not the kind of hands to choose a flowery stationery, to dot each *i* with a tiny heart or scrawl a fanciful flourish underneath his name on the cover.

Not the kind of hands to dress a kid in ruffles and red velvet, two sizes two small, and dump her off at a stranger's hotel. The woman who had dressed the kid and written the letter was not the type to wear baggy khakis and a flannel shirt over a stretched-out turtleneck pullover, her hair in a tangle and a streak of dirt across one cheek.

Because hunting fugitives, some of whom had successfully remained hidden for years, happened to be his business, Mac had developed a built-in radar system. Everything about this woman was blipping like crazy, yet all he could think about was how come a woman could dress like last year's scarecrow and still manage to look elegant, poised and too damned attractive for comfort?

Something didn't fit. He was beginning to take it as a personal affront. Lies and evasions were an everyday part of dealing with the kind of people he was forced to deal with. But for reasons that escaped him, he resented being lied to by Banner Keaton.

"Look, let's make it easy on the kid, shall we? You level with me, and we'll work together to straighten this mess out. If you're planning to remarry and the guy's not interested in a ready-made family, there are agencies that can help." He had to force the words out. He couldn't bring himself to look at her, because if that was the case, then he'd like nothing better than to wring her delicate, swan-like neck!

"Mr. MacCasky—"

"Ford."

"Make up your mind. I don't know what sort of game you're playing, but I assure you, I am not amused. That child is not my daughter, and how she came to be in your hands, Lord only knows, but I pity her."

"You and Keaton didn't have kids?"

He could practically hear the key turn in the lock as she said, "My personal life is no concern of yours. Please remember that you're here on my sufferance."

Ignoring her last sentence, he said, "Ah, but you're wrong. Your personal life is exactly why I'm here in the first place, remember? Now, as I said before—if you're having personal problems, help is available. I'll even steer you through the channels, but you're going to play it straight with me. No more lying, no more running. That's the deal I'm offering as of this minute, but I warn you, lady—I've had one hell of a week, salt air doesn't agree with me and I'm on a short fuse, so make up your mind real fast."

Waiting, he watched her like a hawk. It was rare that MacCasky found himself backed into a corner. When he did, he usually chose one of two options: fight or negotiate. He lacked the stamina to fight. Even against a woman who looked as if a hard sneeze would blow her over.

It would have to be negotiation. Unfortunately her very first move had tipped the odds in her favor there, too. How could a guy play hardball with a woman who fainted at her first sight of him?

Which was another thing he needed to get to the bottom of. What ailed her? What would it take to fix it? What kind of support system did she have—because it was obvious she needed someone to help her.

Not him. Oh, no, not him! He didn't owe her a damned thing!

A small movement behind him had him reaching for the Beretta he wore tucked under his belt in the hollow of his back.

The kid wandered back into the room and took her chair. He hadn't even noticed when she'd slipped away. She could barely see over the table, and Mac found himself wanting to lift her up onto his lap. At the same time he wanted to protect her from men like himself, men who had lived rough for too long to be trusted with something so small, so sweet, so vulnerable. He was way out of his depth and sinking fast!

Struggling to hide her growing uneasiness, Banner divided the hot chocolate into three mismatched mugs and then added more honey to her own. She needed the quick energy boost. The past six months had been unusually stressful, and today she'd been pushing hard to finish up here. She'd put off eating, which probably explained why she'd embarrassed herself when she'd jumped up to go open the door.

Trying to ignore Mac Ford's cold scrutiny, she slid the pot of soup over the burner and then placed the three mugs on the table.

"Don't burn yourself, darling," she cautioned the child. "I can add some more milk if it's too hot."

The little girl shook her head and sipped noisily, darting a wary look at the two adults. Banner thought she looked adorable with a milk moustache. Could she possibly be... Banner knew that Rory had had a girlfriend. He might even have remarried after their divorce. She'd made it her business to get as far away as was practical once she'd recovered from losing her baby.

This child had his eyes, as well as his name. She'd fallen in love with those eyes nearly eight years before. Deep green, with glints of gold and amber. On Rory they'd been wicked, daring her to follow his lead. On the child they were wary and wistful.

Rory's daughter. But what was she doing here? And who was this great gray eagle who was guarding her so fiercely and accusing Banner of lord knows what crimes?

"You want to read the letter or not?" The great gray eagle flicked the pink envelope that still lay where she had dropped it.

"It's not addressed to me."

"Read it," he commanded, and reluctantly Banner removed the single sheet from the envelope. "Would you mind telling me who you are first?" she asked.

"I told you—my name's Mac Ford. In case you've forgotten, this is Tiffany Eleanore Keaton."

"Eleanore," Banner repeated. "That was Rory's mother's name."

"She also happened to be my mother." He didn't bother to add that he'd lost any claim to the woman nearly thirty-one years ago, when she'd walked out, leaving behind a shell of a husband and a shattered young boy.

Turning to the child with a gentle smile, the woman asked, "Are you called Tiffany? Or Eleanore?" When there was no response, she said, "Then I'll call you Ellie, if I may?"

To Mac's amazement, the kid actually smiled. It was the first time that had happened since she'd landed on his doorstep, so to speak, two days before.

Suddenly it struck him that women—even fledgling specimens like the half-pint—had an unfair advantage over their male counterparts. The child's smile was having an effect on him, and he wasn't sure he liked it. Wasn't even sure what it was.

But the effect of the Keaton woman's smile was a little too specific for comfort. Not to mention totally inappropriate. Knowing little more about her than her name, he found himself fantasizing about unbuttoning her blue flannel shirt, peeling off that stretched-out pullover and stripping those baggy khakis down over her legs. Was her skin the same shade of creamy vanilla all over? Or was it even paler? And the color of her hair—that shade that was neither red nor brown—was it natural?

MacCasky had always trusted logic up to a point. When logic failed, he went on pure instinct. Logic told him he was on the wrong trail. Instinct told him he'd better get the hell out while the getting was good.

Ignoring them both, he hitched his chair closer to the table and settled in for the long haul.

Two hours later, feeling reasonably satisfied of body, if no more satisfied of mind, Mac carried the sleeping child up a narrow stairway to a dimly lighted bedroom under the eaves, wincing as his healing knee protested even the slight additional weight.

The predominant smell was of mildew and some faint, imperceptible sweetness that he couldn't quite identify. Curious, he glanced around him, still holding the child. Age had darkened the paneled walls and plank floors so that a small oval rug and pale quilt on the narrow bed glowed luminously in the light of a single oil lamp.

An assortment of pots and bowls were placed, seemingly at random, around the floor. Now Banner moved past him, emptying one of the smaller ones into a larger one. "At least it doesn't leak over the bed," she said quietly.

Mac nodded. The few personal articles lying around—a hair brush, a thick bathrobe, a book and that faint, intriguing scent that seemed to be a combination of spice, orange peel and sunshine—told him that the room was her own.

She folded back the quilt, and he tiptoed across the room, his boots sounding unnaturally loud against the heart-pine floor. "From the way the wind's cutting up out there, I wouldn't count on staying dry anywhere," he warned as he lowered the limp body onto the narrow mattress. Gently he smoothed Ellie's white-blond hair back from her forehead. Seeing his own hand against her small pale face, he was moved.

And he didn't want to be moved. Couldn't afford to be. "I guess it's been a hell of a day for the poor little devil," he muttered. "She really lit into that soup. Packed it away like she hadn't eaten for a week."

"Maybe she hasn't."

"Don't kid yourself, lady—I watched her put away a slab of beef and a couple of pounds of fries last night, and then top it off with a banana split big enough to choke a hog."

Of course, she'd lost it all, too—in the middle of his bed, while she was watching television. He didn't bother to mention that, but he'd fed her enough since then to make up for it. The kid was a bottomless pit.

From the shadows near the foot of the bed, Banner studied him silently, taking in the shock of thick, steel gray hair, the irregular features, the gaunt frame, softened by the warm glow of the kerosene lamp. At one time he'd probably been considered strikingly handsome. Now he looked merely tired and worried. She could almost imagine a look of concern in those deep-set eyes of his.

And then she reminded herself that looks could be deceptive. Especially by lamplight. From now on when she looked at a man—*if* she looked at a man—she'd prefer it to be under the harsh glare of cool white fluorescents.

Abruptly she turned toward the door and beckoned for Mac to follow her out. "Turn the wick down, but not all the way out," she whispered. She didn't want to admit it, not even to herself, but there'd been something oddly touching about the way he had gazed down on the sleeping child.

Instinctively she sought to analyze it out of existence, telling herself it was only the contrast between the delicate child and the tall, rough-hewn stranger. Something about the man got on her nerves.

Or maybe it was the island that was affecting her—being cooped up here in the dead of winter, without another soul around. For all the happy summer vacations she'd spent here, winter was something else entirely. She'd found that out when she'd come here with Rory on their honeymoon.

But this was no honeymoon, and MacCasky Ford was no Rory Keaton. Whoever and whatever he was, he was no concern of hers. "I'd better leave the door open a crack so we can hear her if she wakes up."

"Hear what?" Mac shot back. "Have you heard anything out of her so far?"

"She obviously has a problem. Is it physical or—"

"Come on, let's go back downstairs first."

They headed for the kitchen. Banner had filled the kettle after supper and left it to heat. Now she poured hot water into a gray graniteware dishpan. "I'll wash while you fill me in if you don't mind. There'll be enough water left over for another cup of tea afterward."

Tea! What he needed was Scotch. Or at least coffee, hot, black and strong. During his late great incarceration, the food had been scarce and largely unpalatable, but the coffee had been terrific. If you happened to like the kind of coffee you could eat with a knife and fork, and Mac did.

While she swished up a lather and placed the scraped dishes into the water, Mac assembled, sorted and discarded all but the most pertinent of the questions he'd come armed with. He watched silently as she squeezed out a cloth and washed off the wooden table, ignoring him, but not being mean about it.

He liked the way she moved. He liked the way she looked. He'd always been partial to women with the kind of quiet, understated beauty that allowed a man to discover it by degrees. Ten years ago—or even two—he might have done something about it.

Not now. With his body looking and feeling like something that had been unearthed from the bottom of a landfill, about all he could handle for the foreseeable future was holing up somewhere off the beaten track and trying to deal with the fact that every sound, every shadow, every unexpected movement, no longer threatened a quick and permanent end to breathing.

He could handle that, but there was no place in his life for a woman, except for an occasional temporary liaison. He didn't need anything more, he didn't want anything more, he didn't believe in anything more.

"You wanted to talk?" he challenged.

"I thought you were the one who wanted to talk," she returned in that unflappable tone of hers.

Feeling his blood pressure begin to rise, he deliberately took a deep breath. "At your convenience, ma'am."

At the undisguised sarcasm in his tone, she shot him a searching look and then deliberately turned away and continued to wipe off countertops and burners. Scowling, MacCasky watched her move quietly and surely about the barren old kitchen, finishing her chores. Unsought images began to form in his mind—images he lacked the energy to resist.

The kitchen was warm and steamy by now. She'd removed her shirt and shoved up the sleeves of her yellow cotton pullover, revealing the soft, smooth skin of her forearms. As she leaned over to place a pot under the counter, the worn seat of her pants slipped over her backside like a caressing hand, tracing curve, swell and valley. The soft knit of her shirt fell away from her body, faithfully revealing the slope of her back. He could even see the shadow of her spine, and the faint indentation where her bra cut into her flesh.

Absently Mac unbuttoned the second button on his own flannel shirt. Damn! Surprising how a single kettle of water could heat up a room like this! Belatedly it occurred to him that the instinct he'd relied on to keep him alive had fallen down on the job.

"Okay, first question," he said curtly. "What are you doing here?"

Startled, she lifted her head to stare at him. After a few seconds she went on with her work. "I'm washing dishes," she replied with a calmness that sent his blood pressure soaring again. "Before that I was helping put a child to bed. Before that I was—"

"Cut the crap, lady. It's getting late, and I'm in no mood for a comedy routine."

The look she gave him then made him vaguely ashamed of himself. Somewhere along the line he'd managed to pick up a few principles, among them that women, while not necessarily to be respected, were never to be abused. "Sorry. I meant, would you mind telling me why you're here in a place like this by yourself?" It galled him that she could make him feel this way without even trying.

"I was packing away books I want to take back home with me. Before that I was—"

"All right, I can do without an itemized itinerary," he said, "Cut to the chase. Who exactly *are* you? Why did you lie to me? Where is—"

"I told you who I am. My name is Banner Keaton, and I do not lie," she said firmly.

"You admitted you were married to Rory Keaton."

"I *told* you I'd been married to Rory. I didn't 'admit' anything. There's a difference, you know. If it's of any interest to you, I was also divorced from him." With maddening deliberation she rinsed a handful of stainless-steel flatware and upended it into a drainer.

Divorced. Okay, so his old man had missed a clipping, and Conner's team hadn't picked up on it. Or maybe they had, only Mac hadn't stayed around long enough to find out the details once he'd got a lead.

"So you're divorced. Where does the kid come in?"

"You tell me."

"What do you know about Keaton's other women? Were there any? What about another wife? Did he remarry?" Mac knew he was leaning on her too hard, but something told him that if he didn't get to the bottom of this business and get out of here fast, he was going to regret it. So he'd push her for everything she knew, and then he'd get out. "Well? We can drag this out if you want to, but I'd just as soon wind it up tonight."

"Not that I'm aware of, but then I didn't keep up with my ex-husband after we parted. If you have any more questions, I suggest you save them for someone else. I've told you everything I intend to tell you."

He suddenly saw that she was furious. Maybe she had a right to be, but dammit, something told him she was holding back—something he'd seen in her eyes, something he'd sensed earlier.

When? If he could remember what had been said at the time, maybe he could put it together, but he was too tired to go after it tonight.

Sprawled in the green straight chair, he gazed up at her, his thoughts, his questions, his suspicions well hidden behind half-closed lids. She met his eyes with a disconcertingly level look. Nothing evasive about her now.

He almost wished she'd screech at him, curse him—throw something at him, but even mad as hell, she was determined to behave like a lady.

Suddenly the walls began to close in on him. Raking back his chair, Mac moved restlessly to stare out the window. He rubbed a clear place on the steam-dulled windowpane. It was pitch-black outside. The wind was howling like a soul in torment. From behind him came the clink of stainless steel against the graniteware dishpan as Banner Keaton began to scour the soup pot.

He drew in a deep, ragged breath. Wind, rain and kitchen noises. The lingering smell of corned beef hash, tomato soup, lemony detergent and burning lamp oil.

A quiet, brown-eyed, russet-haired woman, cool to the point of being passive. A woman with the kind of face that made a man want to look beneath the surface—to discover what had put that hint of sadness there. That made a man want to find out if she'd come apart in his arms, under his naked body, or if she'd remain cool and passive there, too.

MacCasky swore under his breath. Somewhere along the line he'd screwed up. Again. Either that or the Keaton woman was a world-class liar. And although it galled him to admit it, something in that steady gaze of hers told him she was on the level.

It would have been easier if she'd been what he'd expected—*who* he'd expected. He'd spent a lot of years dealing with lowlifes in all sizes, shapes, colors, nationalities and genders. He'd learned all the tricks in the book, and written a few new pages.

But women like this one were a different matter. How could he uncover what wasn't hidden in the first place? Was she holding something back, or had he only imagined it? Where did he go from here?

"Will you tell me something, Mr. Ford?"

"Try me."

She poured boiling water into a pair of mugs and dropped two tea bags in his, one in her own. "Why are you looking for Ellie's mother? Can't you simply look after the child for her? She'll be back, you know. Women don't give up a child—not that easily."

Mac felt a minor blip on his internal radar. It was in a location where there shouldn't be a blip, but it was there, he was almost certain of it. "You read the letter. She gave her up, all right, because she had a better deal." Mac knew all about women who gave up their kids because they had a better deal. All his sensors were out now, but nothing was registering. He was tired. It would keep. He had her on the run now, he thought with quiet satisfaction.

"You'll have to stay here, you know. I'd already packed away all the linens but those on my bed, but—"

"The bed you gave the kid."

She nodded. "Call her by her name, Mr. Ford. I expect she needs all the recognition she can get, being handed over to a stranger who obviously can't wait to get rid of her."

An expletive just slipped out. "Sorry," he muttered. "It's been a long day."

A hell of a long day. A long year, in fact.

The bed was damp, the bedding was damp and Mac tried to find a position that was halfway bearable. He'd slept in a lot worse places, and been in a lot worse shape, but he'd been younger then.

Rolling over to ease the pressure on his shoulder, he added up everything he knew for the third time since he'd gone to bed, factored in the things he merely suspected and came to the same conclusion. Banner Keaton might have been married to Rory Keaton, but she was not the mother of his child. Those two had no history together, good or bad. He'd be willing to swear to that.

Dead end. Back to the beginning, to a lead that was growing colder each hour.

Rubbing his shoulder—the one with the shrapnel scar the size and shape of a wedge of cantaloupe—he thought over all the questions he could have asked and hadn't, and dismissed them in favor of the only one left to ask: Would she keep the kid for him until he could get this mess sorted out?

Because he knew he wasn't going to hand her over to the authorities the way he always had before whenever children were involved in one of his cases. Unfortunately, escaped felons sometimes had kids. Fugitives turned out to be family men, and when their women were involved, too...

Dammit, it stunk. When had the world turned into a lousy sewer?

Too tense to sleep, he sat on the edge of the bed, absently stroking his aching shoulder. He'd been given the single bedroom downstairs. It should have been dry, but evidently the rain blew in under the eaves and ran along the rafters until it sensed a victim below to drip on.

At the sound of a creaking board overhead, every muscle in his tired body stiffened. She was awake, too. Or maybe it was the kid....

Should he go upstairs to see?

A drop of cold rain hit the floor and spattered on his bare foot. Resignedly he stretched out again, shifting until he found a dry area approximately three feet wide and six feet long.

He hoped to hell she was having a better night than he was, because tomorrow he was going to tackle her about keeping the kid. He'd get it all settled before the old guy came to ferry them back to Ocracoke, and then, once he was clear of encumbrances, he could put in a couple of calls. Five minutes of computer time would give him all he needed to go on. After that it would be footwork. His footwork. On his time. His hard-earned, much-anticipated free time.

How had he gotten involved in this mess? What if the kid's mother decided on a permanent change of address? What if she couldn't talk this creep she'd run off with into accepting her daughter?

She'd handed her over to him. He was some sort of relative, if you wanted to get technical about it. Which he didn't. And while it probably wasn't legal, he was left holding the bag. The bag in this case being a permanent, pint-sized dependent.

Hell, he couldn't even manage his own life, much less look after a kid! What did he know about kids? Nothing. Less than nothing!

Suppose Banner Keaton agreed to keep her. What if she got attached to the kid, and the kid to her, and the two of them wanted to sew it up all nice and legallike?

What if the mother showed up after a few years and took her away?

What if Harrison Keaton started sniffing around, wondering what had become of his grandchild? Did he even know he had one?

Somewhere in the middle of a dozen or more what ifs, Mac fell into an exhausted sleep.

Four

Staring at the pantry shelves, with their rows of rust-speckled cans, many of them without labels, at the few remaining jars of homemade pickles and preserves, relics of bygone summers, Banner allowed her worries to rise to the surface momentarily. How long before the wind would drop? How long before the boat could come for her? What in the dickens was she going to feed that child—not to mention the man?

Not that she felt compelled to feed MacCasky Ford. Or Ford MacCasky, or whatever his name was.

Snatching up a can that she was fairly certain contained peaches, she slammed the door shut, twisted the wooden button and stalked back into the kitchen to fill the kettle. She could think after she'd had her tea. No point in trying to figure it all out before then, because with the wind out of the northeast and the tide already covering the backyard and standing under her house, she was going to have all the time she needed for thinking.

Too much time.

MacCasky appeared in the doorway, the sharp angle of his jaw somewhat softened by a heavy growth of beard. "The half-pint's still—"

"Her name is Ellie," Banner said evenly.

"Her name is Tiffany Eleanore." Mac held up a hand, palm out, in an unspoken plea for peace. "All right, all right—Ellie, then. Anyhow, I looked in on her, and she's still sleeping. Is that good?"

"It's the best we can hope for. Breakfast is going to be a problem, and that's only the beginning, I'm afraid."

Moving stiffly in deference to his most recent injuries, Mac examined the old-fashioned pitcher pump some whimsical soul had painted in swimming-pool colors. He shifted his attention to the window, staring out at the unremittingly bleak surroundings. He was down to his last three cigarettes, which he fully intended to ration until he actually saw the boat pulling up to the dock. "I'd kill for a cup of coffee," he muttered. "What kind of problems?"

Irritated by what she saw as his selfishness, Banner picked up a small jar and slammed it down on the kitchen table. "Here. Now all your problems are solved."

He scowled at the jar. It looked as if it had been through the wars. "Instant?"

She shrugged. She'd remembered throwing an old jar in the garbage the first day she'd been there—and, of course, the garbage would have to go back across the inlet with her, as there was no place for it on the island. "It's petrified, but maybe you can boil it loose or something."

"If it's genuine high-test caffeine, I'll settle for gnawing it out of the jar." He held the stained and peeling label up to the dim light coming through the tall window. Banner could almost find it in her heart to be sorry for him when his shoulders sagged. "Decaf," he said dispiritedly.

She wielded the can opener, sniffed suspiciously at the contents of the large can and then slid half a dozen juicy peach halves into a bowl. "Now...what goes with canned peaches?"

"Warm goat cheese, a shot of kirsch and a pint or so of espresso on the side."

"I was thinking more in terms of cereal," she said dryly.

He shrugged, and for the first time she noticed how very broad his shoulders were. He had struck her as excessively thin the night before, but she saw now that he was lean. Not thin. There was a difference, one she found oddly unsettling.

"Cereal would be just fine if I had any," she told him, opening near-empty cabinets to stare inside, as if she might have missed a box or a jar hiding behind the slender partition. "Unfortunately I wasn't counting on houseguests. Or this wet northeaster. And cereal doesn't keep very well in this climate, even if the mice don't discover it."

"Yeah. Well...at least the rain's stopped. How long before it runs off?"

On her way to the pantry to see if one of the old cans held hominy grits, which might conceivably double for cereal in a pinch, Banner glanced over her shoulder. "Before what runs off?"

"The rain." Mac had pried the lid off the coffee jar and was inhaling the contents, which were roughly the consistency of asphalt.

"If you're talking about the water in the backyard—"

"And the front," he put in.

"Already?" She sighed. "That was fast. I hate to tell you, but it's not rain, it's tide. There must be a low-pressure area hanging off the coast, and if the wind holds like this, the tide will back up in the creeks and marshes until practically the whole island's under.''

Hooking a chair with one boot, Mac dropped onto it and rested his throbbing head in his hands. "In other words, we're trapped in the middle of a flood," he said flatly.

Banner slammed the can of what she hoped was hominy down onto the counter and attacked it with the can opener. "No, we are not trapped in the middle of a flood," she said through clenched jaws. "The tide is *slightly* higher than usual because of the wind and—and how the dickens do I know why? I'm no meteorologist. If you don't like it here, you shouldn't have—Ouch!"

She jammed her bleeding forefinger into her mouth and flung the dull can opener into the sink. For two cents she would walk out and leave him to sulk and whine till he turned blue, but as much as she'd like to, she could hardly go off and leave that poor baby upstairs.

Not that she even had a choice.

"What did you do to yourself?" he growled, looking as though he hoped she'd whacked off a limb at the very least.

"Nothing!"

Rising stiffly, he blocked her escape, trapping her neatly between the pie safe and the counter. "Let me see, woman."

She jerked her hand behind her, feeling threatened in a way that confused her. "It's nothing, I told you! Anyway, it's no concern of yours. Just because Rory was your—"

"Banner." The taste of her name on his tongue was shockingly intimate. He swore under his breath. Reaching around her, he caught her hand and held it up for examination.

Banner gave in ungraciously to his greater strength. His hands were long and surprisingly graceful, for all they were hard as iron. Banner drew in a deep breath and then wished she hadn't. To her amazement, even the scent of him was disturbing. Last night he'd smelled leathery, outdoorsy, masculine. She'd marked it down to the sheepskin-lined coat.

This morning he wasn't wearing the coat, yet the essence of him was even more masculine—to the point of being threatening.

"It's just a scratch," she murmured, keeping her eyes downcast.

"You stabbed yourself. If you'd get a decent piece of equipment—"

"I *had* a decent piece of equipment!" Using her free hand, she yanked open a drawer and pulled out a chunk of rusted metal attached to two yellow plastic handles. "This is what happens to decent equipment down here. At least on the one I was using, there were no moving parts to rust solid."

Lord, what was happening to her famous serenity?

She tried to tug her hand away, but those long, square-tipped fingers formed a gentle manacle that held her in place. The force of his gaze shone down on the top of her head, generating enough heat to make her uncomfortable.

Uncomfortable? She was terrified! He was a stranger. He had a gun—she'd seen it in his belt once when his back was turned, although he wasn't wearing it now. He could be a kidnapper or an escaped convict, yet within hours of arriving on the island, he was making her feel things she'd sworn never to feel again!

Well, she wouldn't. A long time ago Banner had learned how to deal with unwanted feelings. Denial. It was as simple as that.

She drew in a deep, uneven breath. "If you'll excuse me now, Mr. Ford, I'll finish what I began and then go upstairs. If Ellie wakes up alone, she might be frightened."

"First put something on that finger."

She risked a glance at him and discovered that he was still too close. She could see all the way into his eyes, and what she saw there disturbed her even more than his touch did. "Yes," she whispered, never breaking eye contact. "Finger? Uh, peroxide..."

Mac watched her hurry from the room. Gradually he became aware of his surroundings. Of the cold damp draft that leaked in under the back door. Of the noise the wind made keening around the corner of the house, whistling through the misshapen tops of cedars and live oaks.

Shaking his head, he limped back to the kitchen table. If he didn't get off this island, he'd be in worse shape than that yellow-legged can opener of hers.

Banner Keaton...Mrs. Rory Keaton, he mused. Damned peculiar, the way she got under his skin. She wasn't even particularly pretty. If she had a figure, she was determined to keep it a secret.

Once again he found himself wondering what she would be like in bed.

And wondering what the hell he was doing wondering.

Listening to first one and then two sets of footsteps overhead, MacCasky rubbed his temples with his thumbs and tried to get his derailed train of thought back on track. Why couldn't the broad have headed for the desert? Somewhere hot and dry, where he could bake his carcass until it began to mend again?

He'd been worked over, shot up, whacked open and otherwise spindled, folded and mutilated so many times in the past fifteen years that nothing was ever going to work the way it used to. His warranty had run out years before.

He should have handed the kid over to the authorities and headed for the hills when he had a chance. Now it was up to him.

At his best, MacCasky knew he was no diplomat. Mix in a high level of frustration at having messed up again, a rusted-out body and a five-alarm caffeine withdrawal headache, and you had a real prince of a guy. How the hell could he sweet-talk her into going along with his plans?

The kid wasn't with her when she came back downstairs. "Ellie's getting dressed. She prefers to do it alone."

Mac glanced up, doing his best to ignore the effect her voice had on him. Calm. That was the word that came to mind when he looked at her. Even her voice was sort of calm and peaceful—that is, when she wasn't chewing him out. "She tell you that?"

"Not in so many words."

Leaning back, he dropped his gaze to the worn linoleum on the floor. "Yeah. I figured. Look, I'm sorry if I flew off the handle. This thing has got me in a real bind."

Banner dug out a chunk of the petrified coffee and poured boiling water over it. Handing him the mug, she sat down across the table. "I can understand why you're so worried. She's such a precious little thing, it's hard to believe any mother would give her away like that."

"Legally I'm not sure she did." He thought he'd better get that part in now, before he asked her to look after the kid while he went after the real mother. Unless he missed his guess, Banner was the type to get attached to anything small and helpless. He didn't want her hurt when this thing was over.

A slight sound from the doorway alerted them, and they both looked around to see Tiffany Eleanore, her corduroy jeans on backwards, her striped knit shirt wrong side out, and her brand-new pink-and-white sneakers on the wrong feet.

"Hi, darling," Banner greeted, rising swiftly to go to meet the child. "I'll bet you're hungry, aren't you? I've planned an adventure for us this morning. Instead of ordinary old cereal and toast, we're going to have lovely peaches and a nice bowl of warm hominy, and if you'd like, we can spoon a little bit of honey and cream over the hominy. Would you like that?"

Solemnly the child nodded her head. Mac noticed that her hair had been brushed and tied back with a shoestring, a vast improvement over his own efforts of the day before. He tried to rise too quickly and fell back again. Cursing silently, he used the windowsill and the table for leverage and stood up.

They'd warned him back at the hospital that if he didn't go in for a regular course of therapy, he'd be lucky ever to regain full use of some of his favorite muscles. Eager to hole up on his farm where he could make a fool of himself without an audience, he'd promised to follow the therapist's instructions to soak his muscles and exercise.

He'd have promised to learn to play the flute if it would have got him out of that three-ring circus one day sooner.

Now he pulled out another chair and lifted the child up beside him. "Morning, half-pint. Did you get rained on last night?"

She stared up at him, and Mac found himself wondering what secrets lay behind the shadows in those big green eyes. Over the child's head Banner met his gaze, and a feeling of communication flowed between them, startling him with its intensity.

"Yeah, well . . . maybe after breakfast you can help me empty the pots and pans under the leaks, okay? If Miss Banner's a good girl, we might even let her go upstairs and help us."

Green eyes glistened. A dimple hovered momentarily at the corner of a small rosebud mouth, and Mac felt something clamp down hard and tight inside him.

He had to get out of here. The sooner the better.

The breakfast of hot hominy grits and canned peaches wasn't the worst meal he'd ever had, but it was far from the best. Ellie loved it. She polished her bowl and stared at Banner wordlessly until she offered her what was left in the pan. Silently Mac commanded his own half-empty belly to shut up and be grateful for small favors.

He made himself a mug of strong tea and laced it with canned milk and sugar. It wasn't half-bad. At least it provided his deprived body with a jolt of genuine caffeine.

After the breakfast things were cleared away, while Banner washed the dishes, Mac and the child went upstairs and emptied the leak catchers out a back window. Ellie sloshed more onto the floor than went outside, but Mac ignored it. He never remembered either of his parents letting him get away with anything. He'd been taught that regardless of age, each person was responsible for his own actions.

But a child this small—a child whose father was dead—a child who'd been deserted by her only remaining parent, deserved a break.

Mac found himself wanting to gather her up in his arms and shield her from the world. He wanted to tell her everything was going to be all right, only he couldn't promise her that. No one could.

Instead, he ushered her back downstairs without saying anything. Dammit, he refused to get involved! She didn't need him; she needed someone who could love her, someone who would be around tomorrow and all the tomorrows that came after that.

Personally MacCasky didn't believe in love. If love was what his mother and father had shared, then it was a sucker's game. If love was what his mother had felt for her seven-year-old son when she'd gone off and left him with a bitter old man, then he wanted no part of it.

Hell, he wasn't sure he even believed in tomorrow. He was no good for the kid. The sooner he handed her off to someone who still had a few illusions left, the better off they'd all be.

"We need to talk," he told Banner a few minutes later as she put away the last dish.

To his great relief, she didn't argue. "I have some books."

They settled Ellie at the table with a box of ancient second-and third-grade readers. Mac glanced through one and saw the name "Pearl McNa," with "ir" written on the following line. It was dated 1928. The cover said it was a second reader. "*Hiawatha? The Town Musicians?* I don't remember my own second reader having three- and four-syllable words."

"You were probably a year later than Great-Aunt Pearlie," Banner remarked without a glimmer of a smile.

"Maybe even two." He shot her a suspicious look. Hadn't the woman ever seen prematurely gray hair before? Turning his attention to the child, he bent over her and leafed through a few dog-eared pages. "Lots of nice pictures, half pi—uh, Ellie. Maybe I'll read you a story later on, huh?"

"I'm sorry there's no fire in the front room," Banner said when they left the warm kitchen. "I burned all the paper trash yesterday. There's probably wood out in the shed, but it'll be under water by now."

"I'm warm enough. What about you?" Two mugs of scalding tea had helped him considerably. His head still ached, but his joints were beginning to function reasonably well.

"I'll be all right." She was wearing layers again. White turtleneck, blue chambray shirt, and a man's brown pullover with holes in the elbows. Arms clasped over her breasts, she settled into an ugly rocking chair, leaving him the iron-upholstered slab of a sofa.

Mac did the gentlemanly thing. "You want to go first?"

"Why don't you start at the beginning and tell me everything?"

Amusement twisted his lips briefly. "Okay, I'll go first if you insist. The kid's—"

"Ellie."

"Like I said, Ellie's mother skipped out and dumped her on me."

"You're a relative."

"That's stretching it. I never even met my half brother. All I know about him is what I read in the newspapers."

"Why?"

He frowned. "Why? Hell, how do I know? Because a seven-year-old kid doesn't have a lot to say about things, okay? Because two weeks after my mother left us, my old man loaded up the truck and we took off. In eleven years I attended twenty-three different schools. Does that give you some idea of how much control I had over my life?"

"You grew up." She stated the obvious and waited for his reaction.

"Yeah. I grew up. From the time I was old enough to read, I used to check the phone book in every new town we settled in, looking for an Eleanore Ford. After a while I quit looking. I'd wanted to find her for the old man, not for me. Personally I didn't give a good damn. Pa never mentioned her name, though. At least, not to me."

Her silken brows lifted, but she said nothing. Mac shifted so that he wouldn't be facing her. It was easier to talk that way. And for reasons he couldn't understand, he felt compelled to talk about things he hadn't discussed with anyone, not even Conner Jones.

"Pa used to say we'd go back to the farm in Wilkes County as soon as he'd made enough to fix the place up. He was a builder by trade, but he had a hair-trigger temper and a heavy thirst for beer. Maybe he didn't start out that way—I don't remember. Anyhow it was a bad combination for holding down a steady job."

"Do you think he knew Eleanore had remarried?"

"Yeah, he knew. He'd known all along, only he hadn't thought it was any of my business, I guess. Oh, hell, I don't know—maybe he thought he was protecting me or something. Anyhow, when he died, I found an old scrapbook full of clippings. Eleanore Ford's marriage to Harrison Keaton of the Virginia real-estate Keatons. There was one a few years later that showed her opening a new shopping center he'd built, and then there was a birth announcement—Rory's. Five pounds, three ounces. Scrawny kid. I weighed in at eight-two."

For some reason he grinned.

For some reason she smiled back.

Mac shook his head. "I don't know why the hell Dad saved all that stuff. They used to fight like cats and dogs, even when they were together."

"Maybe he missed her," Banner said softly.

"Yeah, like I miss caffeine, Scotch and tobacco. Even if he did, why'd he keep all those old clippings about her boy? Rory was nothing to him."

"I don't know. What about the things you were doing?"

The look he gave her was genuinely puzzled. "What things?"

Staring at a faded photograph she'd left framed on the wall because it seemed to belong more to the house than to any one family, Banner said, "I know the sort of things Rory did—the auto races, the stunt flying and all that. Surely you did *something* that made the papers."

Yeah, Mac reminded himself—he'd done something, all right. He'd made the papers on several occasions, only his name was seldom attached to the deeds. He'd done the job he'd been hired to do, and done it well up until recently. "Not much, I guess," he said aloud.

"Rory was jealous of you, did you know that?"

It took a moment for the words to sink in. "The hell you say! He didn't even know me!"

She smiled, but there were shadows lying just under the surface. The same shadows he'd noticed yesterday. "He knew more about you than you think. Eleanore kept up with you. I don't know how, because she died a year or so before I met Rory. He used to talk about you, though. He thought you were some sort of international spy. Kind of a James Bond. I don't know if he made it all up or not."

Mac bit off a crude retort out of deference to his audience. "I hate to disappoint you, but if that's what he told you, he was a mile wide of the target. Until a few days ago I was a federal marshal. Not one of the guts-and-glamour guys. Not CIA or FBI or Delta Force, just a plain old garden-variety marshal."

"Weren't Bat Masterson and Wyatt Earp U.S. marshals?"

"Yeah." He grinned crookedly. Gazing at the battered cowboy boots he'd bought in Dallas to celebrate an occasion he'd long since forgotten, he missed the look of relief on her face. "So was Matt Dillon, for that matter, but this is real life, not a TV series. And in real life, we marshals are the low men on the totem pole in the justice system. Most of the work is tedious, boring and repetitious. Occasionally it's dangerous. It's a job," he said with a shrug that was one-sided and not entirely convincing.

"Rory played at being a man," she said softly. "But he could never have done what you do. And I happen to know something about the marshals. I read an article once—"

She'd read an article. Mac uttered a short laugh. He'd read an article on brain surgery once, but he didn't know any more about it now than he had before he'd read it.

"Look, that's not important," he said. "*She's* what's important." He nodded toward the kitchen, where they'd left Ellie with a box full of books. To his amazement, Mac realized the truth of his words. She *was* important to him. Somewhere along the line she'd become more important to him than anything had been in a long, long time.

And that was *not* a good sign.

"Your turn," he said with the uncomfortable feeling of having exposed far more of himself than was comfortable—or even safe.

"There's not much to tell." Her hands had been resting in her lap. Now she lifted them, flipping them palm over in a small, graceful gesture that Mac found utterly captivating.

"Tell it anyway," he said gruffly.

"You know I was married to Rory, and I told you we were divorced. That was five years ago—nearly six now."

Mac did some quick mental arithmetic. She'd said Ellie wasn't hers, and he had to believe her. Everything he'd seen had borne that out. Which meant that Keaton had probably been running around even before he'd divorced his wife. Score one more against love. Or against marital fidelity.

"He had a girlfriend?" he asked aloud.

"Several. No one special—at least not while we were together. Or not that I know of."

"Would you have known?"

"He'd probably have told me. Rory always liked to brag."

Mac's headache took a turn for the worse. He was liking his late half brother less and less. "The note said the kid's name was Tiffany Eleanore Keaton. Would some bimbo have made that up?"

Banner shook her head slowly. "I don't know. Would it be legal? The name, I mean."

"I guess a woman can name a kid whatever she wants to. Makes her harder to track down, that's all. There's no telling what name's on the birth certificate. Tiffany Eleanore could have been born in the lobby of my hotel."

"But why?" Banner's large eyes widened distractingly, and it took Mac a moment to realize what she was asking.

"Money. That's usually the case. If some creep waits a few weeks until we get real attached to the kid and then comes out from under his rock with an offer to sell her to us, that'll be a pretty good clue."

Banner leaned forward, resting her elbows on her thighs. She seemed to be wrestling with something. Did she know more than she was letting on? All his instincts leaned toward trusting her, but experience told him he couldn't trust his own shadow, much less some strange woman.

"Mac, she's Rory's daughter, I'm almost sure of it. It's the eyes. His were the exact same color."

"That could be a coincidence, or it could have been planned that way. Green-eyed kids aren't all that rare."

"Yes, but it's more than that. I just…feel it. I think she really is his daughter, but as to who her mother is, I haven't a clue." She closed her eyes as if she were in some kind of pain, and Mac looked away.

He had to believe her. Dammit, he didn't want to, because it would have been easier if she'd been the right one. But there was something about Banner Keaton that made him trust her.

That was a first. A dangerous first. "Okay, so she's his," he allowed.

"And yours," she reminded him. "That makes her your blood kin."

"Jeez," he said with a sigh. "You don't pull your punches, do you, lady?"

"Why else would the mother have picked you out when she could have given her baby to almost anyone? How did she find you?"

That one was easy. She'd seen the media smoke screen the agency had laid, recognized his name and found out where he was staying. "Who knows? The thing is, she did."

"Yes, but—"

"Look, let's cut to the bottom line," he said, breaking in. "The important thing is finding whoever left her with us—"

"With *you*."

His cool gray eyes gave away nothing. "All right, with me, then. But I can't very well go after her unless you'll agree to—"

"Take Ellie off your hands."

He had the grace to look embarrassed. "Yeah, well...would you? I don't mean permanently or anything like that. I'll find the woman, it's only a matter of time."

"How can you be so sure? Shouldn't you turn the problem over to the police? There are social workers who—"

"You want me to turn that baby in there over to a bunch of strangers?"

"Keep your voice down. I only meant that you're not a marshal any longer. You said you'd retired. There are other people who can find a missing person, and there are other people better able to deal with Ellie's silence. Or hadn't you noticed that she doesn't talk?"

Shoving himself up off the sofa, Mac began to prowl. He felt trapped by more than the weather. "Don't push me, woman. I retired for personal reasons, not because I'm past it. As for Ellie's problem, I don't think a few more days is going to matter that much, do you?"

Banner didn't know what to think by now. She did know that MacCasky Ford was too forceful, too intimidating and perfectly capable of pushing her into something all her instincts warned her against getting involved with.

She had every reason to hate this child. She was Rory's child—the child he hadn't wanted with her. The one he'd given to another woman.

Dammit, it wasn't right! What if she got attached to Rory's daughter and then had to give her up? She'd already lost one baby. Could she go through the pain of losing another one?

MacCasky had been pacing. Now he broke into her thoughts, and she gave them up willingly. She wasn't getting anywhere. "Look, you're a woman, aren't you?" he reasoned. "She's a decent kid. Quiet, obedient—she won't give you any flak. I'll be back for her before you know it."

He was limping. She hadn't noticed that before. There wasn't a whole lot of room in the house to move around, or perhaps she might have. "Suppose I agree?" she ventured.

He came about too quickly, and his knee buckled. It was not a graceful landing, but at least he made the couch. If he'd landed on the floor at her feet, she would have been embarrassed for him—but not nearly as embarrassed as he would have been.

Somehow, without knowing how she knew, Banner was certain that this man had a great deal of pride—and that it had been severely tested at some time in the past. His quitting the service probably had something to do with his injury.

"Damned wet floors," he muttered, although the floor was perfectly dry. "Look, if it fouls up your personal plans, I'm sorry, but I can't go chasing all over the damned country looking for a baby-sitter! I need to get on with the hunt before it's too late."

"Too late? You mean—"

"I only mean that a cold trail's harder to follow than a warm one. You'll do it, then?"

She sighed. "I don't have a choice, do I?"

Banner tried to meet his gaze, but he seemed fascinated by the claw feet of the old cast-iron stove. Clearing his throat, he said, "It's not as though you were a total stranger. I mean, you and Keaton were married. She could have been your kid, but for the luck of the draw."

Feeling as if someone had just pressed the air from her lungs, Banner gripped the arms of the old rocking chair until her knuckles whitened. The luck of the draw? Was that what it was? Rory had fathered two children—two that she knew of. One had lived and one had not. Luck of the draw.

"Banner?"

Her eyes seemed to look right through him, and Mac wondered if she were going to faint again. She'd said that the first time was only because she'd forgotten to eat, but maybe... "Banner, are you all right? Come on, lady, don't look like that. If you're going to get sick, give me some warning first, huh?"

Ignoring his protesting muscles, Mac crossed the room and went down on his good knee beside her. "Hey, what is it? Just because I said a little rust on the outside of the can never hurt anyone, you don't have to go this far to prove I was wrong."

Gradually her eyes seemed to focus again. She even managed a small chuckle, and when Mac reached out and covered her shoulders with his hands, it seemed the most natural thing in the world for her to topple forward until she was resting her forehead against his shoulder.

"Forget it. I always react this way to low barometric pressure," she said. "At least I promise not to rain all over your shirt collar."

"Was it something I said?" He was only half joking. Something had triggered that stricken look. He might be slowing up in some areas, but his eyesight was still twenty-twenty.

When she didn't answer, he forced himself to his feet again and stood over her. "Come on, let's go back to the kitchen and check on our kid—she's probably cleaned out the pantry by now. Never saw a logger's appetite come in such a small package before, did you?"

Five

Staring out a front window, Mac summed up the details of his forced incarceration. Day three. Wind still high but falling, rain dropped off to the occasional drizzle, tide beginning to go down.

If there was one thing he'd had enough of to last him a lifetime, it was confinement. Even confinement with an attractive woman. Here there were no strong-armed orderlies, no scruffy, underage guards armed with top-of-the-line automatic weapons, but there might as well have been. Not even in his salad days would he have attempted to swim the inlet. In the shape he was in, he wasn't even sure he could make it on foot as far as the dock.

As for the amenities, he had a damp, lumpy bed, no heat, three cigarettes and not a damned thing to drink stronger than tea, instant decaf or pickled peach juice. To date, he had eaten potted meat on limp, mildewed crackers, preserved citron on more of the same and something from a rusty can called creesy greens. He'd had worse food. But not a whole lot worse.

Ellie had polished off every scrap. By mutual consent they had saved the choicest cans for the child. Tonight he'd choked down the last of his canned greens while the half-pint had feasted on sardines and cherry pie filling.

Slapping his shirt pocket, Mac reassured himself that his precious hoard of tobacco was still intact. By now it was probably mildewed, like everything else in this seagoing mausoleum.

"Mac? Do you want anything else from the kitchen before I blow out the lamp?" Banner called softly from the back part of the house.

"Yeah. Could we talk over a cup of tea?"

"Why not? We've talked over everything else."

He grinned in the darkness and levered himself up off the hard couch. In the three days since he'd met Banner Keaton—two and half, to be more precise—he had come to appreciate things about her he'd never even noticed in other women. Her quiet sense of the ridiculous. Her patience under trying circumstances. Her calm resourcefulness.

The way she had of nibbling on her bottom lip when she was worried, the way her lashes drooped when she was sleepy, as though they were too heavy to be supported by her shadowed lids. The thick glossiness of her hair, her utter lack of artifice and the scent of citrus and spice that seemed to cling to her clothes and skin.

Day three. God help him if he had to spend many more days imprisoned on this forsaken scrap of dune and marsh alone with a woman like Banner Keaton. Not that he'd written off women altogether. Just because he didn't believe in commitments, that didn't mean he didn't believe in women. But he was in no shape to deal with any kind of woman right now—at least not the way he wanted to deal with this one.

"How's your headache?" Banner asked as he walked stiff-legged into the kitchen.

He shrugged. "Not bad. The tea helps." It might cauterize his gut, but at least it delivered a mild jolt of caffeine. As for the rest of him, he was feeling more like that yellow-legged can opener of hers every day. Rusted stiff and useless.

"I found some aspirin, but they smell sour. I expect they're too old."

"I'll survive. The kid asleep?" he asked as he reached for the kettle. Banner had placed two mugs on the table, dropping one bag in hers, two in his.

"Like an angel."

"I didn't think angels ever slept." He filled both mugs, refilled the kettle under the pump and replaced it on the propane stove for morning.

"Of course they do—it's in their contract. Insomnia is reserved for the candidates who don't make the grade." Her smile said she knew all about sleepless nights.

So did MacCasky. "How soon do you think we can get out of here?"

"Probably by tomorrow afternoon. The wind's dropped off enough so you can hear the surf again. It still sounds pretty rough."

Tomorrow. Day four. Damn!

Mac squeezed out his tea bags, field-stripped them into compost and garbage and tossed the tags into the bag of trash she was collecting to take back with her. Earlier she'd washed out the day's cans and he'd flattened them, not trusting her with the can opener.

"Any milk opened?" he asked. She'd forgotten to put the can on the table, and he shoved back his chair and rose, grabbing the edge of the table when his knee threatened to buckle under him. He cursed, and Banner stood and pressed him back down. "Sorry, I forgot. We're on the last can of milk, by the way."

Great. So now he'd be taking his tannic acid straight. "Never mind," he growled as she placed the can and the honey pot on the table in front of him. "I'm getting used to the stuff."

"Mac, I don't mean to meddle, but I couldn't help noticing that you—that is, your—well, anyway, when I was looking for aspirin, I came across a bottle of lineament in the medicine cabinet. I don't know how old it is, but it might be better than nothing at all."

"Instead of canned milk? Lady, I've tasted some strange beverages in my time, but—"

"For your leg. That's what's bothering you, isn't it?"

His leg, his back, his shoulder—and at the moment, his head. In more ways than one. "Thanks. I'll check it out." Taking a sip of the hot black tea, he grimaced and then scowled when she began to smile.

"Go on, finish the canned milk. It won't hurt Ellie to do without for a day or so. Lord knows, she gets enough variety in her diet, even if some of it's pretty weird. There's bound to be calcium in some of that stuff we feed her."

"Have you decided yet?" It had been on his mind almost constantly—whether or not she would agree to keep the child while he went after the mother.

"Whether or not to take her home with me, you mean?" she said softly. She wasn't a woman to mince words. He appreciated that.

"I can't very well take her with me, and if I turn her over to the authorities, that's the end of it," he countered. "I'd never get her back."

"Do you want to?"

Her eyes gleamed darkly in the lamplight, and Mac found himself trying to read her. There was still a hell of a lot he didn't know about the woman called Banner Keaton. The important thing was that he trusted her—at least he trusted her to take good care of Tiffany Eleanore Keaton. MacCasky didn't trust too many people in this world. "Yeah," he said gruffly. "Sure...maybe. At least until I find out what kind of woman would dump her on me that way and run."

"The letter said she was getting married."

"Would you choose a man over your own kid?"

Something flashed in her eyes then. As dark as they were, he saw it. Pain? Whatever it was, it was gone almost immediately.

"Some women would, I suppose."

"Some women definitely would," he said, thinking not so much about the woman who had given up her child to a stranger as his own mother, who had simply abandoned both her son and husband.

Banner was silent. Her composure ate at him. It made him uncomfortably aware that he was using her for no real reason except that she was available and Ellie liked her. Kids had an instinct about these things, he told himself.

"She needs you," he said, wanting her to commit herself.

Dammit, *he* needed her! And if that meant manipulating her, he wasn't above such tactics. He didn't have a whole lot of choice if he wanted to keep the kid from getting trapped in the relentless gears of the social welfare bureaucracy. "Banner, she needs you," he said again more gently.

"No, Mac—she needs someone, but I don't think I'm the right one. I can't handle it by myself."

All expression left his face as he leaned back in his chair, both large hands cradling the big, chipped mug. "Naturally I'd expect to pay for your services."

She was furious. Color flared in her pale cheeks, and her eyes glinted like live coals, but her voice, when she spoke, was low and even. "I wasn't speaking of the financial part, although there's that, too. She needs a specialist, and she wouldn't be covered under my health insurance policy. Besides, when I go back to work, I'll have to find someone else to look after her, and—" She broke off, her molasses-colored eyes pleading with him. "MacCasky, she needs more than a baby-sitter. The child can't talk! I don't know if it's physical or mental, but whatever it is, she needs professional help, and I can't give it to her."

"You think I don't know that?" he shot back. Leaning back in his tilted chair, his clear gray eyes narrowed to thoughtful slits, Mac studied the woman seated across from him. Had he called her calm? She fired up quickly enough on behalf of the kid, but even then, she simmered down almost immediately. What was it with her, anyway? What did it take to get under her skin?

She fascinated him. He didn't know why. God knows, she didn't dress to catch a man's eye, but still she intrigued him. "Level with me, Banner, are you okay? Physically, I mean?"

Two blinks and she'd caught up with him. "Because I fainted, you mean." Her lips pursed in the center and lifted at the corners into a puckish smile, and he stared at them, totally captivated. "I'm not the swooning type. The day you showed up, I'd tackled the worst of the mess to be sorted through. I'd skipped breakfast and forgotten to eat lunch, and then, when I jumped up to answer the door..." She shrugged.

He sent her a skeptical look, more to get a rise out of her than because he doubted her word. She rose so beautifully once he managed to get to her that he couldn't resist.

Cheeks flushed, eyes blazing, she said, "I'm healthy as a horse, for goodness' sake! Didn't you ever jump up too fast and get dizzy?"

He surprised himself by chuckling. "Not recently."

Abruptly she stood and carried her mug to the sink. "Now, is that all, or do you want my shoe size and the name of my next of kin?"

"Six double A?"

"Six and a half," she corrected. "Is that a part of your training?" Without giving him a chance to reply, she said, "I'm going up to bed now. Blow out the lamp when you come up. Oh, and the lineament's in the medicine cabinet if you're interested."

Halfway up the stairs, her feet began to lag. The man obviously had problems. What if he genuinely needed help?

Of course he didn't. If ever she'd seen self-sufficiency on the hoof, MacCasky Ford was it. If he had a sprain or was getting over some sort of injury, it obviously wasn't severe enough to prevent him from coming here after her.

Or rather, after Ellie's mother.

"Banner?" he called up the stairs, and she turned and waited until he reached the bottom step. He was openly limping now, holding himself stiffly. He moved like an old man, but in spite of his graying hair, he couldn't be all that old. There was nothing at all old about the way he looked at her.

"Did you need something else?" she asked softly.

"Uh...well, now that you mention it, there's this place on my back that, short of dislocating my arm, I can't reach. These past few nights sleeping on a wet, swaybacked mattress must have thrown something out of line."

She nibbled on her lower lip, wondering if she should feel guilty. But dammit, she hadn't invited him here! "All right. I suppose it's the least I can do."

She'd slap some lineament on his back and pray they could all get off the island tomorrow. If he had other ailments, he could take care of them himself.

"I'd appreciate it," he said softly after she'd turned away.

Banner finished up in the bathroom and looked in on Ellie, who was sound asleep, clutching her monkey doll. Next she collected a cotton blanket from the box of linens she'd already packed. By that time Mac was waiting outside his bedroom door, smelling of soap and toothpaste.

"How is she?" he whispered.

"Sleeping. Poor baby, how could any woman go off and leave anything so sweet and helpless?"

"Yeah," he murmured after a moment, and together they entered the dark, cold bedroom.

"I'll light the lamp," Banner offered, but Mac shook his head.

"No point in it. You can see well enough from the one in the hall."

"There's plenty of lamp oil. We may as well—" Banner had already turned toward the dresser when she felt Mac's hand come down on her shoulder.

"Leave it," he said tersely.

Bossy, irritable man! She was sorely tempted to leave *him!* Instead, she opened the hall door wider, propping it with the doorstop she'd made as a child by covering a brick with burlap and embroidering it with Aunt Pearlie's crocheting yarn. There was a mantel lamp on a stand in the hall just outside the door, and she turned it up, spreading a circle of pale yellow light across the satiny plank floor.

For a moment she thought he was going to object to that, but he'd already turned away and begun to unbutton his shirt.

Peeling back the quilts, she spread the folded cotton blanket over the bottom sheet, tucked it under the mattress, noting guiltily that he hadn't been exaggerating—the thing looked like a hammock and felt like a damp sponge.

Next she opened the bottle, consciously averting her gaze as Mac, minus both shirt and undershirt, came to stand beside her. "Will it hurt to lie down on your stomach? We could probably find a board out in the shed to put under your mattress."

"Another night won't kill me. Do your thing."

Not until he had stretched out across the bed, keeping to the near edge of the mattress, did Banner see the scars. It was all she could do to hold back a gasp. His back was muscular, but not grossly so. The fact that he tapered down in a wedge shape to a narrow waist made his shoulders look all the more broad.

There was a large, crescent-shaped scar, darker than the surrounding skin, on his right shoulder. Gnawing her lower lip, she stared at it and then looked away. Smaller scars were scattered in a random pattern, as if he might have taken a load of buckshot in the back at some time in his life.

She groaned unconsciously and saw his right hand slowly tighten into a fist. He said nothing. Pouring a small amount of lineament into her palm, she rubbed both hands together to warm them, staring all the while at the evidence of past violence. He wore his jeans low on his hips, emphasizing a build that was totally masculine. A shadow of dark hair trailed up from below the belt line on either side of his spine, but it was not that that held her horrified gaze.

Someone had evidently dragged a garden rake across his back again and again. She couldn't tear her eyes away. Oh, God, how she wished he'd never asked her to do this! MacCasky Ford had seen more than his share of violence and pain.

"Look, why don't we forget this and say good night? The smell of that stuff alone will probably do the trick."

"No, I—MacCasky, does it—Oh, Lord, I'm sorry. Is there—is there anyplace in particular that bothers you?" she managed to ask when she had her feelings once more under control.

"Right shoulder, down the center, and out from there." He sounded like a man with his jaws wired shut.

"It won't—sting, will it? Are any of these scars fresh?" She prided herself on sounding so matter-of-fact, and then her damned eyes started to water.

Lineament vapors. The stuff smelled to high heaven.

"It's all ancient history, honey. Close your eyes if it helps."

With grim determination she leaned into her job. No wonder the man had quit, if this was evidence of the way U.S. marshals were treated. It looked as if he'd been beaten, horsewhipped and shot at. She, who almost never lost her temper, found herself furious on his behalf.

"Hey, you don't have to work it down into the muscles. A surface application is all I'm after."

"Oh. Sorry." She'd been wondering who could have done such a terrible thing, her stokes growing more and more forceful.

His skin felt surprisingly smooth, considering the way it looked. It also felt hot, but perhaps that was the lineament. But it wasn't the lineament that was causing his muscles to grow tense under her hands. A massage was supposed to have the opposite effect.

This wasn't smart. She should have offered him a hot towel and left it at that.

Her face impassive, Banner leaned over his narrow hips and tried to concentrate on being impersonal, but it was no good. He had a long torso. By the time her flattened hands had reached his shoulders, her own body was twisted uncomfortably.

Mac grunted as her thumbs worked to soften his rock-hard trapezius muscles. Next she drew her hands slowly down his powerful back in a long, firm stroke, thumbs following the valley of his spine. Reaching his narrow waist, she began again, carefully leaning only a portion of her weight onto her elbow-locked arms.

He was stiff. It didn't take a physiotherapist to know that every muscle in his body was as tense as a sheet of glass. "Don't—stop," he breathed as she reached the top of another long sweep.

"I'm not, but if I don't change positions, I'll be the one needing a back rub." Oh, no! Why had she said that? It sounded as if she were wanting to start something, and she wasn't. She most definitely was *not!* "Um—maybe if you were to lie sideways across the bed?"

"With my knees on the floor, you mean? Honey, I'm not even sure they'll bend that much. How about if you climb aboard and straddle my hips?"

She'd brought that one on herself. Cheeks flaming, she continued to rub briskly, ignoring her own discomfort. "I'll manage," she muttered, placing one knee on the bed and twisting to bring herself into better alignment with his long body. "A few more strokes should finish you off."

"Lady, you don't know the half of it," she thought she heard him mumble. But then he said aloud, "Stuff smells like garlic and horse mint," Mac mumbled. "What's it made of?"

"Garlic and horse mint."

"What's the matter, are you afraid to climb into bed with me? I assure you, I'm no threat."

"Don't be ridiculous, of course I'm not afraid. I said I'd spread this stuff on the places you couldn't reach, and I've done it. I *didn't* agree to massage out every kink in your carcass."

"Thank God for small favors. Does the smell ever go away?" he asked, and before she could answer, he'd rolled over onto his side. Catching one of her hands, he dragged it up to his nose.

He was breathing hard, but then, so was she. The whole room reeked of lineament. "Mac, stop it. My eyes are burning. I want to go wash my hands." It was as good an excuse as any. She had to get away—that was the important thing.

One minute she was leaning over his prostrate form, the next, he was on his back, still clutching her wrist, and she was sprawled out across his chest. "You want to settle for two out of three falls, or shall we go for three out of five?"

"Damn you, I will not *have* this, do you understand?"

Her voice fascinated him. It was low, husky and full of subtleties. Still waters. He could feel the undercurrent all the way to his marrow. Suddenly it occurred to MacCasky that he was playing a dangerous game. A game in which he was ill equipped to compete, much less to win.

He let her go abruptly, and she stood up, rubbing her wrist and glaring down at him. Lying half on his side, half on his back, he closed his eyes. "Leave the bottle on the nightstand," he said tiredly. "Thanks for the back rub, Banner. It helps."

For one brief moment she was silhouetted against the light from the doorway, baggy trousers, layered shirts and all. Damn! He could still feel her hands burning into his flesh, and it had little to do with that stinking horse-lineament she'd used on him. He was stiffening up all over again, in places where lineament would be decidedly inappropriate.

What the devil was it about this woman that affected him this way? She wasn't beautiful. She wasn't even par-

ticularly good company. As for sex appeal, he'd turned
down offers while he was still in the hospital from women
who could easily put her in the shade.

So why, he asked himself when the door clicked shut
behind her, was he about to rupture the zipper on his
damned jeans? Why was he thinking about citrus and spice
when the whole house smelled of garlic and horse mint?

Why, instead of a coarse cotton blanket and a layer of
damp quilts, was he still feeling the silkiness of her hair
when it had slithered past his cheek?

Okay, so her wanted her. It wasn't the first time he'd
been turned on by a woman he couldn't have—it probably wouldn't be the last time. It was seldom fatal. The
thing he had to keep remembering was that he needed her
even more than he wanted her. And if he loused up the deal
he'd made with her just because his hormones had chosen
this inconvenient time to kick into action again, then tide
or no tide, he'd be up a creek without so much as a tooth-
pick!

Six

Sometime during the night the wind switched around to the northwest and the sky cleared completely. By daylight most of the tide had gone down, leaving behind acres of tired and beaten bulrushes. Water still stood in the low sections along the sandy road, but from what MacCasky could see from an upstairs window, they looked negotiable, with care.

"I've opened the last three good cans," Banner announced when Mac joined her in the kitchen. He'd hoped she would be still in bed. He needed a stiff jolt of caffeine, preferably laced with nicotine, and enough time to work out just what he was going to say to her. Nothing had been settled conclusively about whether or not she would take Ellie home with her. He couldn't much blame her for not wanting to get mixed up with him and his problems.

"So?" he said cautiously.

"What would you like for breakfast? Canned greens, sliced beets or ripe olives?"

He'd been staring without meaning to. She was wearing the same outfit she'd had on that first day, and it hadn't improved with age. Her hair was tied back with a shoestring, the mate to the one she'd used on the kid. She looked feminine, strong and fragile all at the same time. It made him hurt in places no lineament could reach.

"What about the kid?" he mumbled, forcing his eyes away from the pale oval of her face.

Classic. He'd heard the word applied to a woman's beauty before. Now he knew what it meant.

"I hope she likes popcorn for breakfast," Banner said with a hint of a smile. "I found half a jar on the top shelf."

"What are our chances of getting out of here by noon?"

"So-so. If Rosie comes across, she can call Captain Julius and have him pick us up, but even if she can't make it, he should be showing up pretty soon. He knows I'm expecting him."

"Why can't this Rosie person take us across the inlet?"

"For one thing she's not supposed to be a ferry service. For another she comes from the opposite direction. She's headquartered in Beaufort—we're going to Ocracoke. They're in different districts."

"Let her get territorial on her own time, I've got to get out of here."

Without answering, Banner took down a large aluminum pot and placed it on the burner. She wrestled with the lid on the popcorn jar until Mac removed it from her hand and unscrewed it for her. "I like extra butter on mine," he said, and she gave him one of those calm, sweet looks of hers that drove him right up the wall.

By early afternoon it was clear that neither the park ranger nor the guide would be coming for them. With the hard northwest wind had come a steady drop in temperature that could become a problem. The inlet was once again too rough for small-boat traffic, and Banner had no idea how much propane was left in the tank.

"What about the coast guard?" Mac asked. He was prowling like a caged animal—which wasn't far from the truth.

"I'm a little surprised Captain Julius hasn't sent them to check on us. Rosie probably thinks he picked me up before the storm. She doesn't even know about you and Ellie."

Mac frowned at the evidence of increasing wind outside—the blowing rushes rippling like waves across the marsh, the twisted live oaks, the noisy palmettos that raked circles in the sand beneath them. Dammit, he had to get to a phone! A cold trail was tricky as the devil, even if no one was trying to cover it.

A lot depended on how smart the woman was, and how determined she was to disappear. And, whether or not the experts would admit it, Mac knew that a lot depended on luck.

That was the hell of it. A multibillion-dollar network, years of training and more years of experience, and all of it could come down to a matter of sheer luck. Something no man born had been able to define to his satisfaction.

Luck.

Mac's narrowed eyes lingered on the woman who was calmly putting together another meal from the dregs of nothing. Was it luck that had brought him to this deserted island in the middle of nowhere? Was it luck that had made him take off on a wild-goose chase without checking out all the possibilities?

"Did you tell Captain Julius who you were?" Banner asked as she tossed together beets, olives, vinegar and pepper into a breakfast salad. The corn began to pop.

Without breaking her rhythm, she reached across the front of the stove with one hand and lowered the heat. All her movements were like that, he thought with reluctant admiration—economical, efficient and as graceful as any dancer's.

"Huh? Oh...sort of," he said when he remembered her question.

"What kind of an answer is that?"

Mac eased his long legs out straight and gently kneaded the muscles above his knee. Unbidden, an image flashed across the screen of his mind, and he saw her small, capable hands stroking the spasming muscles of his thighs. Switching off his imagination, he asked, "What kind of answer were you looking for?"

She ignored him. The corn smelled faintly burnt. It was popping halfheartedly, the kernels probably too old and too damp to do much more. She slid the pot off the burner, removed the lid and stalked out of the room, her back expressively rigid. Evidently she didn't care for smart mouths.

Great. Now he was stuck here with a kid who couldn't talk and a woman who wouldn't.

As if to punctuate his irritation, one last kernel of corn popped out of the pan, landing on the floor a few inches from his foot. Mac stared at it, wondering what was really eating at him. The feeling of being trapped was nothing particularly new. He'd learned in tougher schools than this to deal with confinement and stay sane.

It was the woman. For some reason she got under his skin. When he was with her, he couldn't take his eyes off her. When he wasn't, he couldn't get his mind off her. That sense of calmness, of serenity that surrounded her, as though she moved in her own little world, ate at him. Made him want to rattle her cage, just to see if he could get a rise out of her. Or maybe just because he hoped some of what she had would rub off on him . . . God, he didn't know!

It was probably just the weather. He'd been through harmattans in West Africa, khamsins in Egypt, samiels in Syria and siroccos in Sicily.

So now he knew the effect of a low-pressure cell hanging off the Outer Banks of North Carolina.

A reluctant grin creased his lean face as he wondered what the scientific world would make of his symptoms. Restless, irritable, aching joints—and horny as hell!

"—and if you eat all your popcorn, Mr. Ford will take us up some oysters," Banner was saying as she entered the kitchen. "Have you ever had oysters rolled in cornmeal and fried nice and crisp? They're delicious!"

Oh, great. Oysters. Just what he needed.

"Are you sure you want to do this?" Banner asked for the third time an hour later. Bundled up, the three of them were standing outside the weathered net shed, which was leaning approximately thirty-degrees off square.

"I'm not sure of anything," he grumbled, trying to keep his teeth from chattering. "Hell, I'm not sure I'll even recognize an oyster in the wild."

"You agreed to go."

He sent her a sour look. "I seem to remember getting volunteered for the job."

"The oysters here are wonderful. I'd forgotten about them."

"Pity you got your memory back. Ah, hell, I'm just kidding, honey—I like oysters. The kid'll probably love 'em."

"I can go," she said, her words nearly swallowed by the sharp gale that whipped directly into their faces off the water.

"I said I'd do it," Mac snapped. "The ancestral waders would swallow you whole."

"Are you sure you don't want the coat, too? You could tuck it into the top of the waders."

"Keep it. Maybe we can use it to patch the roof if it rains again before we get away from here."

"You have an extremely negative attitude, MacCasky, did you know that?"

"It's one of my more endearing qualities," he growled. Taking an experimental few steps in the ancient waders, he headed for the water.

Banner, her usual layers topped off with the stiff, rubberized coat they'd found hanging in the shed along with the pair of old waders, stood in the shelter of the building with the child tucked under her coattail. Ellie had wanted to explore the cluttered shed, but Banner had put her foot down. Nor would she let her play on the beach—not until it had dried out. Well she remembered from her own childhood how the sand could give way unexpectedly after a tide or a hard rain.

MacCasky glanced back at the pair of them, and they waved. Feeling slightly foolish, he waved back. Hail the conquering hero.

Funny how quickly those two had learned to communicate, he thought. Female intuition? Whatever it was, it left him feeling like an outsider. It was baffling, the way Ellie would look up silently and Banner would nod or shake her head in answer to an unspoken question.

Of course, he told himself as he slogged through choppy water up to his knees, it might not be the right answer to the right question. Still, both of them seemed satisfied.

Before the water had even reached his thighs, Mac knew that the waders were in the same condition as everything else on this forsaken place. He felt the icy trickles at the back of his ankles first, and then suddenly he was soaked up to his knees.

He came close to turning around right then and there. Only a fool would go wading on a day when the wind-chill factor hovered around ten above. But one look at the pair waiting for him on shore, and he made up his mind to fill his damned basket full of oysters if it crippled him!

So now he'd be wearing wet pants for the rest of his stay. That was just great! He'd brought along his shaving kit, chiefly because it was a good place to carry extra ammunition. At the moment his gun was there, too, in a lidded, white enamel bucket under the bed. Everything else he owned in the world was locked in the trunk of his car back at Ocracoke.

Two big birds flew past, hanging low in the sky. He thought they were ducks, but he wouldn't swear to it. He'd never hunted—at least not wildfowl.

How much farther did he have to wade? How was he supposed to see the things underwater?

The stiff, rubberized canvas gloves she'd handed him at the last minute had never been designed to keep a man's hands dry, much less warm. If they managed to keep them from getting shredded on oyster shells, he'd be lucky.

God, his feet were cold! No—his feet were numb. It was the rest of him that was freezing. The boots, half-full of water, weighed a ton. If he thought he could do it without coming to grief, he'd shed the things and take his chances barefoot, but—

Was that a rock? It was sure as hell no fish. And there was another one—and another.

Some thirty minutes later Mac slogged ashore, the wire basket half-filled with oysters. More than once he'd jabbed his hand with the screwdriver he'd brought along to pry the little devils off the thickly encrusted tires. He hadn't even realized it until his hands had begun to thaw out, halfway back to shore.

Banner was waiting at the edge of the water, her arms wrapped around her slight body, her hair flying wild in the wind. "Oh, good! I was afraid you wouldn't be able to find them. The tide's carried away most of the tires by now, I guess, and some have been covered over with sand." She reached out to him, and Mac had to restrain himself from walking right into her arms.

It was the basket she was reaching for. "Lady, these things had better be good," he grumbled. Handing over the dripping wire basket, he shed his gloves and leather coat, and with numb fingers began unharnessing the leaky waders.

Banner was showing Ellie the oysters, letting her touch one. "In the spring," she said, "When the baby oysters are swimming around looking for a home, people put out old tires and concrete blocks, and the babies fasten onto them and grow there. When they're big enough to eat, we take them off to make room for more oysters to grow."

Mac turned away. Leaning against a dead tree, he began peeling the stiff, dry-rotted rubber down his legs. Awkwardly he tried to work his feet up out of the boots, but suction was working against him. The damned things refused to let go!

"Let me help," Banner offered, and suddenly she was there beside him. She had slipped off her raincoat and wrapped it around the child, and before he could stop her, she was kneeling before him, taking the heel of his boot in one hand, the toe in another.

She twisted. Mac winced. Head down, she persisted stubbornly until suddenly the heel came away from the sole, dumping gallons of water over both of them.

Mac swore. Banner gasped. Ellie giggled, and they both turned to stare at her.

Eventually the small party made it back to the house with their bounty. They left the boots where they had fallen. Banner was even wetter than Mac was, and after one look at her shivering body, he removed the coat from Ellie's tiny shoulders and draped it around Banner's.

"Run along, kid. You can open the back door for us," he said, and Ellie ran, a smile still teasing the corners of her mouth.

They left the oysters on the back porch to be scrubbed and shucked later. The first thing they both needed was a hot bath and some dry clothes. The next thing they needed was a stiff drink.

Fat chance on all three counts.

Banner put the kettle on and apologized for the third time, and Mac shut her up. "Look, I'm only sorry you got wet, too. As for me, I was already soaked. You don't owe me any apologies."

"How about for sending you out there in the first place?"

"I wanted those oysters just as much as you did, lady. From the looks of it, that's all the food we're going to see unless we swim for it."

"There were some ducks on the pond this morning. You've got a gun—I saw it." Her level gaze dared him to deny it.

Mac didn't even try. "Aside from the fact that it's probably illegal to hunt on National Park Service property, I don't think a Beretta is rated for wildfowl."

"You mean you couldn't hit one?"

He didn't know if he could hit one or not. He wasn't sure he could stomach killing anything else, not unless it went for him first. And so far no duck ever had.

"Haven't you ever hunted wildfowl?" she persisted.

"I've hunted," he muttered. He'd been pretty good at it, too. Better than most. Taking up a live oyster didn't bother him. Fishing probably wouldn't. Beyond that he wasn't going to commit himself. "Isn't that water hot enough yet?" he grumbled.

"For tea or a bath?"

"Forget it—I'm going to bed."

"You can't. Not without something hot inside you."

Ellie appeared at the back door. She'd left the raincoat on the porch, which was just as well, as it had swept up half the mud and trash on the path to the sound. Staring directly at Banner, she waited expectantly.

"Not in the shed," Banner said firmly, and Mac's jaw dropped an inch. "And not down on the beach, either. Stay in the yard, all right? There's an old tractor in the bushes beside the shed. You can climb on it if you promise to be careful. Thirty minutes—no later. Once the sun goes down, it will be too cold to play outside."

With a sparkling look the child took off, a blur of pink corduroy, pale ponytail and red, down-filled jacket.

"How do you do it?" Mac marveled. He was peeling the sodden socks off his pale, shriveled feet.

"Do what?" The kettle began to steam, and she took it off the burner. "Would you rather have your share on tea bags or in a pan to soak your feet in?" she asked, ignoring his earlier statement.

"Tea," he told her. "How'd you know what she wanted?"

"What else could she have wanted?"

He could think of a lot of things. A decent meal. A pair of gloves. Her mother. He shrugged and said, "Yeah, right."

At four-thirty in the afternoon, they dined on oysters rolled in the crumbs of three stale crackers and fried in popcorn oil, and steaming-hot oyster stew. No seafood had ever tasted better. Jealously Mac watched as Banner gave the kid the last of the broth from the stew. It was nothing more than oysters, their juice, water and black pepper—no milk, no butter, not even an onion, but it was hot and tasty. The kid loved it. He had yet to see her tackle anything she wouldn't eat.

"Lucky for you I didn't burn Aunt Pearlie's old bathrobe along with the rest of the burnable trash. It came in handy."

Mac didn't care to be reminded of what he was wearing. It was big and warm and dry. Unfortunately it was also made for a woman who'd been considerably shorter than he was. It hit him about midthigh. Between the sagging hem of the cotton flannel robe and the top of his sockless boots was a whole lot of hairy leg, including a knee that had been shot up and reconstructed—and then reconstructed again.

"Yeah, well..." he growled, lowering his head to scrape up the last few grains of black pepper in the bottom of his bowl. "My stuff ought to be dry by now. I'll change and help wash up."

"Denim and flannel? Sorry to disappoint you, but nothing dries slower than denim. I doubt if they'll be dry before noon tomorrow." She'd rinsed the salt out of their clothes and hung them out on the line, explaining that she'd have used the propane stove to dry them faster except that she was afraid of running out of fuel.

Banner had made a valiant effort not to stare when he'd stalked into the kitchen in the green-and-lavender-and-white-striped bathrobe, but she couldn't help herself. Instead of looking ridiculous, as most men would have looked in such a costume, MacCasky had looked formidably masculine, his shoulders stretching the worn seams to the limit, and his muscular, hair-covered legs with their shocking scars exposed from shapely midthigh to even shapelier midcalf.

Glowering, he'd confronted her as if waiting for her to laugh. After one swift, all-encompassing look, Banner had wanted to gather him in her arms and comfort him. Which was ridiculous, because he was the last man in the world in need of comfort.

All the same, she'd felt that way just for an instant, and she was afraid it had showed on her face, because even as she watched, his eyes had turned absolutely glacial.

He'd strode past her, his jaw clenched so tightly it was a wonder his teeth survived. "Where'd you put the damned oysters?" he'd growled. "I may as well get to shucking them if we're going to eat anytime tonight."

"I've already done it."

Swearing, he'd spun around, remembering too late to grab the flap of his robe. "Dammit, I *told* you I'd do it! You can't even open a can without stabbing yourself— you've got no damned business tackling a bunch of oysters!"

"It's called a mess," she'd said quietly, trying to put out of her mind the glimpse of powerful thighs and navy blue briefs she'd caught when his robe had swung open.

He'd stared at her as if she'd lost her mind.

"Not a bunch. Onions come in bunches. Oysters, fish and collard greens come in messes."

And then she'd explained that she'd opened the shells the easy way, by scrubbing them and sitting them on a pan in the oven for a few minutes. Mac had subsided, feeling more like a fool than ever.

It wasn't a feeling any man enjoyed—particularly a man who was beginning to want, against all logic, to make a good impression on a woman.

"Mac, I've been thinking," she said now. "We're going to be here another night. Something must have happened to Captain Julius—either that or he thinks that as long as I have a man with me, I'll be safe. His generation would probably reason that way." Her smile was part whimsy, part sadness, and it ate into him like raw lye. "Anyway, the house is getting colder by the minute, and since the only firewood I have is still wet, I'm considering burning some of the furniture for heat. What do you think?"

"I think that cast-iron sofa in your front room ought to burn at least a week." She laughed outright at that, and he savored each note, tucking them away among his few rare treasures.

"There're a couple of wooden apple crates in the pantry I can use for kindling, and then I thought I might start with those two broken kitchen chairs out on the back porch."

"Let me chop any kindling. You do have a hatchet, don't you?"

"I think so. It should be in one of the crates. I'll look."

Banner knew he'd followed her into the pantry. She didn't know he was standing so close behind her when she stood up with the rusted hatchet in one hand. Thrown off balance by his nearness, she might have fallen if Mac hadn't caught her by the shoulders. The hatchet clattered to the floor, fortunately missing both sets of feet.

Neither of them noticed.

"Banner?" Had he spoken her name, or had she only heard it in her mind, the way she heard Ellie's questions?

"What?" she whispered, seeing the network of fine lines that bracketed his eyes, the flecks of gold in his pussy-willow gray irises and the hedge of black lashes that framed them.

The lashes swept down, and she saw no more, because her eyes had closed, too. When his lips touched hers, it was like being hit by lightning. Too powerful to resist—too powerful to even hurt.

He still held her away from him. Tilting his head, he angled the kiss so that she was utterly defenseless against him, and then he deepened it, stunning her with his intensity. With his hunger.

He wasn't brutal. He didn't force her; instead, he led the way. Warm, silken flesh against warm, silken flesh—now nibbling, now sipping, now thrusting with the tip of his tongue, but never forcing her.

Never demanding more than she wanted to give, but making her want to give him everything she was—everything in her power to give.

Banner could feel the heat coming off his body in great waves. There was tension in the way his hands gripped her shoulders. She tried to move closer, but he held her away, and she stiffened, drawing her head back from his.

"Mac?"

"Don't," he said, his voice like the sound of tearing canvas. A shuddering sigh escaped his lips, warming her face, and she stared up at him. His eyes were still closed tightly. His features—she knew them now as well as she knew her own, could have drawn them if she'd had charcoal and paper—had taken on a subtly altered appearance, the angles sharper, the planes harder, the hollows more gaunt.

His eyes opened slowly while she was still staring at his mouth, and she met his gaze and held it, waiting for...

For what? For the life of her, she didn't know.

"I think we'd better check on the kid, don't you?"

The glow of expectancy dimmed inside her. He didn't even sound rattled. Her whole system was racing like a runaway freight train, and he wasn't even breathing hard. Banner told herself she could easily learn to hate a man like MacCasky Ford.

"Why don't you start on the kindling?" she suggested, her voice betraying nothing of what she was feeling. "Just dump the rest of the tools out of the box. I plan to take them home with me.''

"I left your screwdriver on the back porch.'' There was no emotion on his face, none in his voice, and Banner turned away.

"I'll get it now. I'd better go call Ellie inside, anyway. It's too dark to play outside any longer.''

MacCasky watched her go, admiring her outward composure. Did she know there was the tiniest tremor in her voice? An untrained ear would have missed it completely, but he was a pro. She wasn't quite as unflappable as she wanted him to believe, and that brought a smile to MacCasky's face.

Serene? Yeah, she was that—but she was a lot more, besides.

Seven

It wasn't the first mistake he'd ever made, MacCasky told himself as he lay wide-awake in the darkness that night, trying to will his feet to warm themselves. Nor would it be the last. But it just might be one of the more serious ones.

She was old enough to know her way around. She'd been married to a real swinger, from all indications. He'd formed a pretty definite picture of Rory Keaton, and Banner just didn't match up. Funny, he thought now... he couldn't see the two of them together.

What had attracted her to him? What lay beneath all that sweet reasonableness of hers? Could she be the reason Keaton had gone over the edge?

No. He didn't believe that. Whatever she was, whoever she was, she was good with the kid. That was all that really mattered....

Wasn't it?

Shifting to ease the persistent ache in his shoulder, Mac wrestled with his conscience. So far the score was zip to zilch. The woman had treated him decently—probably better than he deserved under the circumstances. A gentleman would have done the decent thing and left her strictly alone. But then he was no gentleman. And for all he knew, she was just a damned fine actress. He'd met a lot of those in his line of work.

Okay, MacCasky, give me one good reason why you shouldn't go after any woman who turns you on.

How about, the woman's not interested?

She's interested. You may not be a Rhodes scholar, but you know when a woman's interested. If she doesn't want to go the distance, then you can back off, no harm done.

Then how about this one? Even if it turns out she's willing, in the shape you're in, you'll fall flat on your face if you even try anything more strenuous than a handshake.

No problem—she's seen the shape you're in. There are ways.... Besides, it's not going to happen, anyway, so you may as well get some sleep.

On the other hand, she's here. There's something real special about her. And you're here. And it's been a long dry spell.

Mac was an old hand at manipulating a pinching conscience. His was at least a size and a half too small for some of the jobs he'd been forced to do over the years. Sometimes even the most dangerous fugitives had decent families—families who were as much victims as the rest of society. After a while a man learned to do the job with a minimum of feelings.

Okay, so he'd give it a quick shot. No harm in that, was there? Even for an old crock like him. Maybe he'd wait until this thing was finished—he'd have a little more time and be in better shape to run the chase to its logical conclusion.

Then they could both walk away, no worse for the experience. He'd done it before, a number of times. There'd been a girl in Canton, Ohio, when he was sixteen. She'd been a year older, and the walking away had not been by choice, at least not on his part. The old man had gotten itchy feet, and they'd moved to Mobile, Alabama.

He'd even gotten himself engaged once. Keelie Wicker—face like an angel, body like a dying man's last wish. It had lasted seven weeks, until the night he'd stopped by her apartment unexpectedly and discovered the way she entertained herself in his absence.

There had been others since then, but no one important. No one whose name he could remember a few months later. Or in some cases, a few days later.

He wasn't proud of it, but then he wasn't ashamed of it, either. No woman since Keelie had ever been led to expect more than he had to offer—he'd been up-front about that from the beginning. He prided himself that he'd always been a generous lover, both materially and otherwise, but he'd never again offered any woman a slice of his soul. Never even been tempted to.

It was sheer gut instinct that warned him now that Banner Keaton just might be different from all those other women. Not wanting her to be different—not wanting her to be out of his reach—Mac dismissed the thought.

Tomorrow he was getting out of here, he told himself. He'd go back to the starting line and pick up the trail again, and this time he wasn't going to make any mistakes. He knew exactly where he was going to start, and it wasn't with the bureau of vital statistics.

A glance at the luminous dial of his watch showed it to be thirty-seven minutes past midnight. He'd turned in before ten and lain awake ever since. Impatiently he shoved a pillow under his knee and folded his arms under his head. It was better than sleeping on a wet concrete floor—just barely.

Never a heavy sleeper, Banner was on her feet the moment she identified the sound from the bedroom across the hall. Not bothering to put on her shoes, she tiptoed across the icy floors to the room where Ellie was sleeping and quietly slipped in through the half-open door.

"Shh, darling, it's all right," she murmured as she approached the bedside. The child was crying in her sleep. Soft, slurred "uh-hunh, uh-hunh, uh-hunhs" that wavered off into a drawn-out whimper.

"Mmm-ma, I di'n't do it," the little girl wailed, her small pink lips scarcely moving.

"There now, sweetheart, Mama knows you didn't, it's all right," Banner crooned. Edging her hips onto the bed, she drew the child, quilt and all, onto her lap, pressing the small damp face against her bosom.

They were still seated that way—Ellie silent now except for the occasional sniffle, and Banner murmuring meaningless words meant to comfort—when the hall light was blocked by Mac's tall form in the doorway.

"Trouble?" he mouthed almost silently.

Banner shook her head. "She's still asleep. Bad dream, I think, but Mac..."

She glanced down at the small figure in her arms. She seemed to be sleeping peacefully—or as peacefully as a child could when, for some reason, she was afraid to speak.

Because that's what it was. Fear. Banner was certain, without knowing how she knew. Just as she always seemed to know when the child wanted to go out to play, or read a book, or go to the bathroom, or have a cup of cocoa.

Trust was a fragile and precious thing. Once shattered, it could seldom, if ever, be repaired. Someone—some adult—had destroyed Ellie's ability to trust, and it was going to take more than Banner or Mac to put the pieces back together again.

Mac had stepped inside the room so that once more the lamplight shone across the floor, dimly illuminating the tableau. Banner rose unselfconsciously. With one arm she smoothed the remaining covers back and plumped up the pillow, then lowered the sleeping child and drew the thick layer of covers up under her chin.

For a long moment she stood and watched to see if Ellie was going to wake up, to cry again. But whatever had disturbed her dreams was evidently gone now—soothed away, Banner wanted to believe, by caring arms and tender words.

If only all wounds could be healed as easily, she thought as she tiptoed from the room, waiting for Mac to follow before she closed the door halfway.

"What happened?" he whispered, and she laid her finger across her lips and pointed to the other end of the hallway. It didn't occur to her—or evidently to him, either—that there was anything out of the ordinary in the fact that, in an unheated house in the middle of a January night, they were both barefoot, she wearing pink flannel pajamas and he wearing even less than that.

After the first shocking glance, she carefully avoided looking at his body, most of which was exposed in a pair of navy blue briefs and a short-sleeved T-shirt. "I heard her crying," she explained. "Mac, whatever's wrong with her, it's not her vocal chords. She spoke. I mean, not just the crying, but she actually said words."

She could feel his quick interest, literally feel the tension heighten. Without moving, he seemed to come closer. "What words?"

"'Mama'—at least something that sounded like 'Mama.' And then, 'I didn't do it.'"

"What do you mean, you didn't—"

"No—I mean, that's what she said. Something like, 'Mama, I didn't do it.' Don't you understand? Evidently she's punishing herself for something she thinks she's done. Oh, lord, Mac, I can't bear this—for something so small and sweet and innocent to feel so guilty that she—"

With no hesitation at all Mac reached out and drew her into his arms. With no hesitation she went to him. She wanted him to hold her. She needed comfort from whatever source available, just as Ellie had. And just as the child had responded to her own attempts to comfort, to reassure, Banner responded blindly to MacCasky's strength and warmth.

Warmth? They were both shivering, both freezing in the cold, drafty hallway. The only heat was where their two bodies touched, and suddenly that was burning hot.

It was Mac who put distance between them. A few inches of space—enough to bring her to her senses. "Look, let's go downstairs and heat the kettle. Put on your coat and shoes, and I'll grab a robe and meet you there in a few minutes, okay?" He sounded gruff, kind and quite certain she would do as he asked with no argument.

She was tempted to march right back to her own room and slam the door. It had been years since she'd actually slammed a door. Seven years, to be exact. But she would never get back to sleep, and she was tired of lying awake, worrying about Ellie.

That was the whole reason she'd been so restless tonight, she assured herself—concern for the child. What else could it have been? "Tea," she said firmly. "That sounds like just the thing. I wasn't sleepy, anyway. Too much on my mind."

"Yeah," Mac agreed, a glimmer of amusement in his deep, dark drawl. "Me, too."

Strong dark tea with strong dark honey and no milk was not a particularly sleep-inducing beverage, Banner discovered a short while later. They were seated across from each other at the scarred kitchen table, with the oil lamp at one end, turned low.

Mac nursed his mug of black tea in both hands, and Banner fidgeted with her own. She'd been so full of her discovery that Ellie could speak, but having already blurted out that information, she was having trouble getting the conversation started again.

"At least we know its nothing physical," she ventured. Shifting in her chair, her socked foot struck his and she jerked it back and hooked it on a chair rung. "No touchee," her mother used to say to her when she was even younger than Ellie. "Hot, hot, burn Banner's fingers!"

No touchee was right! Every cell in her body was warning her that she was on the verge of being badly burned, yet she was so drawn to this man.

Why? What on earth was there about this battle-scarred, gray-haired veteran of who knew what kind of action that could induce the kind of feelings that had been growing inside her since he'd first shown up on her doorstep and swept her up into his arms?

She wasn't a fanciful person. She'd been declared frigid, unimaginative, insensitive and unfeeling by her own husband, and he was a man who should know, if experience with women was any teacher.

"So where do we go from here?" Mac asked suddenly, and Banner jumped, wondering if she was all that transparent.

"Go?"

"About the—about Ellie? Have you decided to take her home with you? You said yourself the term had already started, and you wouldn't be teaching for a spell. That means you'll be available, doesn't it?''

"Not exactly..."

"Then what exactly does it mean?" He drained his mug and reached behind him to place it in the sink. Evidently the action cost him something, because even in the less-than-perfect light, Banner could see certain lines deepen on his face. The furrows between his thick black eyebrows, and the deep creases that bracketed his mouth.

Her eyes lingered on his mouth...on that short, sharply curved upper lip and the lower one, fuller, square chiseled, looking hard, not soft, as a mouth should look.

"Banner? What do you mean by 'not exactly'? Have you made other plans?"

She blinked and came back to earth. Really...this late hour, all the excitement...she wasn't used to strangers.... "I have a part-time job. Cashier at a restaurant. You didn't think I could take care of Aunt Pearlie and myself on what I make as an art teacher, did you?"

The lips she'd been watching so avidly suddenly tightened into a hard line. "Dammit, I told you I'd pay you, didn't I? I don't expect you to take on anything like this for the fun of it!"

It was the wrong thing to say, and the wrong time to say it. Tired, cold, hungry and constantly kept off balance by her own emotions, Banner jumped to her feet, knocking her mug over in the process. A stream of warm tea ran across the uneven table to drain onto Mac's lap, and he shoved back his chair, staring down in stunned disbelief.

"My last pair of skivvies. Do you see what you've done, woman? The only dry clothes I own, and now you've poured tea all over them!"

Banner had seen, all right. She'd looked, and then quickly looked away, feeling threatened by so much raw masculinity—wet or dry. "I'm sorry, Mac—it was an accident. I'll see if I can find something else of Aunt Pearlie's, but..."

Her lips quivered, and she covered her mouth with her hand. The thought of that intensely masculine body clad in a pair of her great aunt's pink cotton bloomers, size XXL, was more than she could stand. The bathrobe had been bad enough.

"Laugh, and you're a dead woman," he said darkly.

"I'm n-not laughing, honestly," she gasped, still covering her mouth as she backed toward the door.

He caught her before she could leave the room. One hard hand wrapped around her elbow, and he dragged her against him until she was practically standing on his big, booted feet.

Which might have been a bit more comfortable than the bare, uninsulated linoleum floor. "Mac, I didn't mean anything—it was just—at least you've got on a bathrobe—I don't even have one of those. And if you'd kept the thing fastened in front, your—your—you wouldn't have got so wet."

"You think this is funny."

"I do not! It's not at all funny—it's—" She couldn't hold it in any longer. Eyes brimming with laughter, she looked up. And then slowly the laughter died, to be replaced by something altogether different.

"Because if I thought you were laughing at me," Mac said softly, his eyes holding hers with a power that robbed her of her will and her wits, "I might be forced to do something about it."

"S-something?" she managed to whisper as his face came nearer to her own.

"S-something," he repeated just before his mouth—that hard, hot, chiseled-in-granite mouth—closed over hers.

If the first kiss had been a mistake, this one was sheer disaster. Yet Mac knew he could no more have resisted the invitation of those trembling lips than he could have flapped his arms and flown. Some things were meant to happen—some were not.

But whether or not he was meant to get involved with Banner Keaton, something told him it had been inevitable from the very first.

Her lips parted easily under his assault, making him feel vaguely guilty, because he knew that he was going to make the most of what little time they had—he was going to take what she had to offer and give nothing at all in return. She wanted him now. She was honest enough not to deny it. And God help him, he wanted her until he was aching from it!

But once this night's giving and taking was over, that would be the end of it. He wouldn't be coming back later. Because anything he might have had to offer a woman like Banner Keaton had been burned away years ago, and she deserved a hell of a lot more than the husk that remained.

His hands had found their way under her flannel top, and he stroked the incredibly soft skin of her back. Her breasts were small. He could feel the softness crushed against him, but he wanted more—needed more.

And so did she, he told himself as he slipped one hand in between them to unfasten her buttons.

They were still standing in the kitchen doorway. Icy drafts fingered their way through the old siding, under doors, around windowpanes that rattled in their frames. Mac ignored it. He was burning like a fever from inside out.

"Are you cold?" he whispered, lifting his lips from hers just enough to let the words slip past.

Her breath warmed his cheek, and he thought he felt her smiling. Just to be certain, he kissed each corner of her mouth. Sure enough, it was wider than it had been before. "Hmm?" he prompted. "My bed's not too dry, but if we both curl up down in the hollow under the covers, we might manage to generate a little steam heat.''

She was pressed against him so tightly she couldn't help but know the condition he was in, and it had nothing to do with tea-drenched briefs. It had been a long time since he'd had a woman. The pressures had built to dangerous levels.

Reluctantly Mac forced himself to think about what he was doing. This was not just any woman. This was Banner. This was a woman who hid her wounds, her tenderness, her vulnerabilities, under a layer of calm that would have fooled nine men out of ten men.

Unfortunately he was the tenth. He knew better.

But even knowing he had to have her, he forced himself to give her an out. ''Look, maybe this isn't such a good idea, honey. You're a beautiful woman, and God knows I'm a hungry man, but that's just not enough—not for you.''

At first he thought she hadn't heard him. Her arms were around his neck, and she was clinging to his body, her face burrowed in his throat as she strained against him on tiptoe.

With a low groan Mac buried his face in her hair, inhaling the scent of sweet spice and warm woman. ''Baby,'' he whispered, ''maybe we'd better quit while we're ahead.''

She didn't pretend not to understand him. That cut him even closer to the bone—her innate honesty. ''Why? You do want me, don't you?''

A ragged laugh escaped him, and his hands dropped to her hips. He couldn't prevent himself from grinding her against him—just once. And ah, sweet heaven—once more! ''Considering the evidence against me, I guess I can't deny it,'' he managed. ''But Banner—listen, it's not smart. Not for either of us, honey. You're not cut out for quick and rough, and I'm not good for anything more than that.''

It took almost more strength than he possessed, but Mac made himself put her away from him. He stepped back, and the cold air rushed between them, chilling him more than skin deep. ''Go back to bed now. We can't do much about the kid while she's sleeping, but tomorrow, if I have to swim us across the inlet, we're getting off this damned island!''

Half an hour before dawn the moon rose in a cloudless sky, silhouetting the leaning net shed and a dead cedar tree against the glittering waters of the Pamlico Sound. MacCasky decided he hated the old house that, according to Banner, was called Gideon's Retreat after some long-forgotten ancestor. At the moment it felt more like MacCasky's Defeat.

Under a roof that had been fashioned nearly a century earlier of cedar shakes and patched any number of times since with a wild assortment of materials, three people lay in their separate beds. One slept soundly, whimpering only occasionally in her sleep. Two tossed restlessly, both wondering in their own way how a life could be so changed by a chance meeting of two people who should have come together a long time ago, when things had still been possible—or not at all.

Ellie was seated on the edge of her bed when Banner looked in the next morning, her coat zipped all the way up over the Ninja Turtle pajamas the hotel maid had bought her and her baby-fine hair in white-blond rat's nests all over her head. She smiled, and Banner melted right down to the soles of her feet.

''How long have you been awake, darling?''

A tiny shrug was her only reply.

"I don't know what we can find for breakfast this morning, but there's got to be something left in the pantry. Maybe if we both look..."

The child bounced off the bed and came to her, as trusting as if she'd known her all her young life.

Why? Banner wondered, taking the small hand and turning toward the stairs. How was it possible that a child who was afraid even to speak could come to trust a stranger so quickly? How could any woman turn her back on such a child? Banner asked herself again, as she had done so many times in these past few days.

The grief of her own lost baby had lessened with the years, but at times the memories still hurt. Times like this, when she saw such heartbreaking waste and was reminded again of the emptiness of her own heart, her own womb.

The last thing in the world she was prepared to see as she glanced out the back window next to the pantry door was the sight of MacCasky's tall, sinewy figure. He was barefoot, wearing those disgracefully snug nylon briefs under his sheepskin-lined coat, the entire costume topped off by an old red stocking cap she'd thrown on the pile to haul back to the nearest landfill.

At the moment he was striding up from the soundside, carrying the wire basket half filled with dripping-wet oysters.

She flung open the back door and screeched at him. "MacCasky, you get in this house! Are you *crazy?* It's got to be nearly freezing out there!"

"What do you m-mean, n-n-nearly?" he croaked, shoving past her. His teeth were clicking like castanets. He was wet all the way up to his hips, and his feet had turned a peculiar shade of lavender.

Banner tried to take the basket from him, but his fingers seemed frozen to the handle. "Have you lost your *mind?* What on *earth* made you go out there like that, without even putting on a pair of—"

"Boots?" He managed a frozen grimace that passed for a smile, but she could only shake her head. "I'm not ruining my good-luck boots in salt water, woman, not even for food."

"Idiot," she muttered, wanting to wrap him up inside her heart, along with little Ellie, and keep them both safe and warm.

Which was not only foolhardy; it was downright dangerous!

Switching on both burners, she then adjusted the oven control to its highest setting and opened the door. He had to have heat, and quickly. While the water temperature was nowhere near as cold as the air, January was still no time to go wading barefoot, bare-handed, and all but bare—"Oh, for goodness' sake, couldn't you have said something first? I'd have—"

"You'd have what?" He was practically leaning into the oven, one foot lapped over the other one on the cold kitchen floor.

"Locked you in your room, probably. I'll go get your boots. Where are your socks?"

"Still wet. I stopped by the clothesline to check on my way out."

"Probably just the dew. They'll be dry by the time the sun gets up higher. Sit down—no, don't take your coat off. I'll put the kettle on, and then I'm going up to get a quilt. Ellie, you watch him, you hear? If he tries to move out of that chair, call me."

She left, not waiting for a reply. Mac looked at the child. The child looked at him. She smiled, and Mac closed his eyes. Ah, hell, how did everything get so complicated? He was beginning to wish he'd never escaped from that reinforced goat shed in the Montana Grande!

Eight

The oysters remained on the back porch while Banner did what had to be done. With the kettle heating on one burner, her largest pot filled with water on the other, she left Mac huddled in a quilt beside the oven with Ellie watching him like a tiny, green-eyed hawk.

There had to be something—*something*—she had overlooked in Pearlie June McNair's cluttered pantry! Something besides one jar of anemic-looking grape leaf pickles and half a bottle of cider vinegar.

One canister after another proved empty. No good fairy had visited the pantry and left her a wonderful surprise since she'd last looked. One overlooked can of spaghetti and meat balls—was that too much to ask?

"Sorry, the cupboard's still bare," she said with an apologetic smile a few minutes later as she poured three mugs of tea—two weak and sweet, one double strength and bitter as gall. "If I had the nerve, I'd break into the park service building. They must have left something behind!''

"You mean there might be *food* on this island?" Mac started to rise, and she pressed him back onto his chair.

"Sit down, you're not going anywhere."

"Hey, if you don't care about me or yourself, then think of the kid," he said. "She's got to have food. I can go for a week if I have to, but a kid that size, she's got no reserves to draw on."

Banner glanced down at the child as she carried the basket full of oysters to the sink and reached for her scrub brush. Dark green eyes, disturbingly familiar, looked back at her, revealing nothing of the thoughts that went on under that cap of white-blond hair.

What was she thinking? About her mother? About finding herself totally dependent on strangers in a strange land? Or about what she was going to have for breakfast? Banner didn't know. There was so much she didn't know, and the answers were becoming more important to her by the minute.

"Lean aside," she said to Mac when she'd filled two cookie sheets with the scrubbed mollusks. "I'll pop these into the oven for a little while, and we'll have baked oysters for breakfast. Sorry I don't have any catsup, but there's a bottle of vinegar in the pantry."

"Right now I'd settle for raw, shell included. Vinegar will be fine. How about you, sprout? Want to try an oyster cocktail?"

Ellie nodded, her smile slightly wary, but willing enough. Over her head Banner met Mac's gaze, his gray eyes suddenly shuttered, her own revealing far too much, she feared.

Ellie didn't seem nearly as enthusiastic over the lightly baked oysters as she'd been over the fried ones, but she managed to eat a few. Banner would have given anything

she owned to be able to offer her a bowl of oatmeal with
raisins and warm milk.

"If we don't hear from anyone by noon, I'm going to
break into the park—" she was interrupted by a sneeze
from MacCasky "—service place," she continued quietly. "Bless you. I'd better check and see if your clothes are
dry yet."

He caught her hand before she could move away. "Hold
on there—if there's any breaking and entering to be done,
I'll do it. Understood?"

"We'll see. Watch him, Ellie. I'll be right back."

The clothes were dry, and Banner watched MacCasky
disappear around the kitchen door with a certain amount
of regret. There'd been something surprisingly satisfying
about having him wrapped in a quilt in her kitchen, barefoot and helpless.

Helpless, all right, she chided herself as he sneezed again
from the next room. About as helpless as a starving gray
wolf.

Mac decided that he was going to live—just barely. At
least if he died—ahh-*choo!*—he would die with his
damned boots on. His headache was down to a manage-
able level, and thanks to the sunshine and the drier northwest wind, his joints no longer felt as though they were
rusted solid. Or no more than could be expected by a knee
that had been shot up and rebuilt and a shoulder on which
a team of surgeons had gone prospecting for scrap metal.

He reached for his crumpled pack of cigarettes, tapped
one out, and then shoved it back in again. If he was coming down with a cold, he wouldn't be able to taste it anyway. Why waste a good smoke?

Retrieving the Beretta from the chamber pot, he shoved
it under his belt and then flexed his shoulders so that his
shirt bloused down enough to disguise it. He hadn't worn

it after the first day. In the house, without his coat, he hadn't felt comfortable wearing it around the kid. Nor had he felt threatened.

At least not physically.

It felt good to be fully clothed again. The first thing he was going to do once he hit the mainland was check into a motel and have himself a long, hot shower. And then soak in a tub neck deep.

God, he'd be glad to see the last of this place!

And the woman, MacCasky—you gonna be glad to see the last of her, too?

He sneezed twice in a row and stalked out of the bedroom, closing the door behind him. There was a farm in Wilkes County waiting for him when this was over. He'd made plans! Those plans had been all that had kept him sane while a grinning runt named Julio had been doing his damnedest to break him.

For one brief moment Mac allowed the memories full rein. Julio had fancied himself an artist with a whip. He could trim a man's beard with it, monogram his hide and do a little minor surgery, all without raising a sweat. As long as the victim was securely bound. Mac had been strung up by his ankles from a cross-arm in an old abandoned silver mine.

Julio's whip had been custom made. It sported a special tassel made of fine, flexible chains with a shot on the end of each one. Mac had felt those tassels on more parts of his body than he cared to remember, but he hadn't broken. He hadn't spilled his guts, he hadn't begged and he hadn't died.

But in the end he hadn't won, either. Julio, from last report, was still alive, recruiting another band of terrorists who knew those mountains, the caves, the passes and ambush spots, as a mother knew her own baby.

"Where's the kid?" he asked, avoiding Banner's gaze as he entered the kitchen. She was cleaning up the mess made by scrubbing the oysters.

"In the front room. I've got a fire going in the stove, and she took her books and your quilt in there." She gathered up a paper full of shells.

"Hey, let me at least do that much for you."

"Fine. You can take these shells out and spread them around the base of the fig tree."

"Fig tree. Uh-huh. Um...what's it look like?" He bundled up the paper full of shells, trying not to let it leak onto his clean, dry clothing.

"Sticks. Like a bunch of brown sticks about head high, at the corner of the cistern."

"The cistern. Oh. Yeah."

She grinned, her dark eyes glowing warmly, and Mac felt another brick in the wall he had constructed over the years begin to crumble. He hurried out the door, and she closed it behind him, her soft laughter following him out.

They were both in the backyard when the park ranger arrived. Mac, sneezing occasionally but otherwise none the worse for his morning expedition, had just dragged a two-wheeled cart out from under a stack of damp firewood.

"I knew that thing was here somewhere," Banner said. "Aunt Pearlie always used it to carry her boxes of groceries up from the landing, and I—Rosie!" She turned to greet the uniformed woman who was just rounding the corner. "I thought you'd forgotten about us."

"Hi. I knocked, but nobody answered—thought I heard somebody talking around here."

Banner gestured to Mac. "Rosie, this is Mac Ford. He's been...visiting."

Mac read the speculation and allowed her time enough to look him over. Then he nodded and said, "Ranger, uh,

Rosie—MacCasky Ford, U.S. marshal. I could use a little help from your branch of service.''

"Marshal?'' The ranger looked from one to the other of them, questions as plain as the freckles on her snub nose.

Mac gave her ten seconds to wonder about the relationship before he said, "I need to contact the mainland, and then we need a lift over to Ocracoke. Two adults and a kid. Can you handle it?''

Rosie explained about the winter schedule and the manpower shortage and the size of her boat, and it was agreed that Mac would go with Rosie to the Dennis Mason House, which served as a ranger station, and gather up any food stores that had been left behind while Rosie contacted Captain Julius.

"Then I'd better get started repacking my boxes," said Banner. "I've dug into several of them, and they'll have to be carted down to the landing one or two at a time.''

"Ellie can help you pack. It'll give her something to do.'' Mac grinned, his eyes crinkling at the corners, and Banner thought what a difference a smile could make. His were rare, and reserved mostly for Ellie.

She sighed, watching the short, round park ranger and the tall, lean U.S. marshal stride off down the narrow, mud-holed path. Authority came in all sizes and shapes. No two people could have been more different, yet she'd come to consider them both friends.

Friends? Was that what she felt toward MacCasky? If she'd been asked to describe the sort of man she liked, the kind she enjoyed being with, MacCasky Ford would fail on every count. He wasn't friendly, he wasn't outgoing, he wasn't open. He had an uncertain disposition, and a sense of humor that was off-beat, to say the least.

Nor was he handsome—at least not by everyday standards. He reminded her of an oyster, hiding its vulnerability and its goodness inside a rough, sharp-edged shell. Hiding its pearls.

"Oh boy! That's what eating seafood for breakfast will do for you, Banner McNair Keaton—too much zinc in the diet softens the brain." Turning back to the shed, she tugged at a length of firewood and tossed it out to dry.

But in spite of her best efforts, MacCasky stayed on her mind while she dragged out the rest of the firewood stick by stick and spread it out in the sun. Buried deep under all those layers of battle-scarred bitterness, there just might be a warm and sensitive man, waiting for the right woman to come along.

It was zinc, all right. She'd known the man for what— three days? Four? So now she fancied she was the ultimate authority on MacCasky Ford, The Inner Workings Of.

"Ha! Big deal!" Grabbing a misshapen chunk of split pine, she hurled it out the door and dusted off her hands, trying not to dwell on the way she had come alive in his arms. That was sheer biology. She'd been married, and naturally a woman of her age had certain—

She dragged out another chunk—oak, this time.

Well, it was only to be expected. That's what all the magazine articles said. She was supposed to be in the prime of her life. Or was that the peak of her powers?

What powers? If she had any powers—peak, prime, or otherwise—she'd never been aware of them. She had "serenity," according to Rory. According to him, her "serenity" had been what he'd needed most in his hectic, adventurous life.

Until serenity had turned to dullness and begun to bore him.

She had loved Rory. Or the man she'd imagined him to be. He'd been handsome, sophisticated, worldly—the kind of man who could easily sweep a shy, small-town art student off her feet.

But once they'd been married and she'd begun to see beneath the surface, he was nothing at all as she'd imagined. Not until years later had she come to realize that the Rory Keaton she had fallen in love with had been largely a creature of her own imagination.

Had she created Mac the same way—out of bits and pieces of fantasy, loneliness and need? Had her overgrown imagination simply latched on to the first tall, lean stranger to cross her path and clothed him in all the qualities she'd ever dreamed of in a man? His potent masculinity had translated into strength. His rare, reluctant smiles, little more than a crinkling of the eyes and a flash of white, slightly irregular teeth, had whispered of hidden warmth and tenderness and all things her life had been sorely lacking in for too long.

Baloney. She hadn't been looking for anything, and her imagination had been in cold storage for years. At least as far as men were concerned.

What's more, MacCasky Ford certainly wasn't pretending to be anything other than what he was. A hard man doing a tough job. A man who had unexpectedly found himself marooned with a woman and a child. So much for that theory.

So why, Banner asked herself as she finished tossing out the last of the wood, did she find herself thinking about him—wondering about him—so much? Why, whenever she was around him, was she conscious of urges and needs that had been hibernating for nearly seven years?

And against all reason, why had something inside begun to stir again the first moment she'd opened her eyes and found herself in the arms of a gray-eyed stranger?

"Because I forgot to bring my vitamin pills, that's why," she muttered, trundling the cart toward the back steps.

"It's a vitamin deficiency—one of the lesser known side effects."

Lord, she was getting more like Aunt Pearlie every day! "Next thing I know," she said with a grin, "I'll be talking to myself."

She took time to put on the kettle before checking on Ellie. The front room was empty, and she called up the stairs. "Ellie? Come on down, darling, I've got some good news!"

Her hands were filthy. She probably had splinters, as well. It took her a few minutes at the sink to wash up, another few minutes to unearth the hand lotion she'd tucked away behind the boxes of dishes she wanted to keep.

"Ellie? Come on, honey. We'll have some tea, and by then Mac will be back with some real food!" That should get her nose out of her book.

Banner smiled as she went about setting out the mugs and the honey pot—she'd have to remember to wash that and pack it before they left. She'd cursed it for years because the lid was just small enough so that, unless it was turned the right way, it fell through the hole and had to be fished out of the honey. But some long-forgotten relative had made it at summer camp and donated it to the cottage. Just lately she was discovering a streak of sentimentality she'd never known she possessed.

"Ellie!"

This wasn't like the child. For all her silence, she was obedient almost to a fault—as if she were afraid of displeasing.

Banner glanced into the pantry, knowing there was little in there to interest a child, and closed the door. Next she checked the closed-off dining room. It, too, was empty. She looked into Mac's room, lingered a moment in the doorway, and then backed out again.

There was a small closet under the stairs, and she looked there next, wondering if the child thought they were playing a game of hide-and-seek. Banner was no longer in the mood to play games. She was even less so after searching every room in the house and finding no sign of a small, yellow-haired, green-eyed child.

Striding along the winding road that led to the path to Gideon's Retreat, Mac told himself he'd made the best deal possible under the circumstances. They'd be spending another night on the island, but at least they had food. And while he hadn't managed to reach Conner Jones, he'd left a message. The wheels would already be in motion by now, and by the time he checked in again tomorrow, he'd know what his next move was going to be.

Next he'd called Ocracoke. At nine o'clock sharp tomorrow morning they were to be collected at the dock on Haulover Point. Approximately an hour later he would be on his way north, and Banner and the kid would be on their way west.

Meanwhile, they could eat.

Banner met him halfway along the path, her shirttail flying, her eyes dark with worry. "Mac, Mac! Hurry—I can't find Ellie!"

Lowering his boxes to the ground, Mac caught her by the shoulders. "Whoa now, slow down. What do you mean, you can't find her? Did you mislay her or something?"

With a surprisingly strong grip, she grabbed a handful of his shirt under the open front of his coat and pulled him toward the house. "Hurry! Didn't you hear what I said, dammit? She's gone! I've looked everywhere, and she's just—disappeared."

"Honey, people don't just disappear. Did you look in the shed? She was wanting to get in there yesterday to do some exploring, remember?"

"I've been working in the backyard ever since you left," she said impatiently. "I'd have seen her! When I was done, I went directly into the house and started calling, and she didn't answer, and—"

"Well, what did you expect?" he asked mildly. "She's not exactly a world-class yodeler." Mac purposefully kept his voice low and even. Banner was on the verge of panic and that alarmed him. In anyone else, he'd have taken it with a grain of salt, but Banner wasn't given to extremes. She was calm by nature, deliberate, not a woman to fly apart in an emergency.

"All right, honey, we'll find her. Is her coat gone? What was she wearing?"

"Oh, no—I didn't even think to look for her coat." Her voice broke, and she covered her mouth with her hand.

Under his deceptively casual manner, Mac's mind was clicking over possibilities, dismissing some, filing away others. A film of sweat formed on his back under the heavy coat, and he ignored it.

Personal involvement of any sort was a hazard, that was one of the toughest lessons any law-enforcement agent learned. Emotions could distort the picture, lower effectiveness. God knows, he didn't need any additional distractions at this point.

"Hurry, Mac, please!" Banner tugged at his hand, her own feeling small and cold.

"Easy, honey. It's not going to help her if you fall apart now." He had to believe that the kid was a survivor, as small and as handicapped as she was. He had to believe that, or his own ability to function might be badly impaired.

For starters, she'd handled being dumped into the lap of strangers and carted off to a godforsaken place like this—handled it like a trouper. The only reason he could think of for that didn't bear reflection—that even strangers who fed her raw oysters and popcorn for breakfast were a hell of a lot better than what she'd come from.

"Do you think—could she have been kidnapped?"

"Now, who would do that?" He wrapped his arm around her shoulders and held her close, although it hampered his walking. "Her father's dead, her mother gave her to me. Who else is there?"

He knew who else—the kid's grandfather. He'd been halfway expecting something to happen, but not like this. Not with no warning. And dammit, not if it was going to hurt this woman. He'd see that old man in hell first!

Mac went through the house quickly, not really expecting to find anything. He searched the shed and then, all the reassurances he spouted out so glibly beginning to taste like mud on his tongue, he surveyed the natural hazards. Marsh, woods, ponds and the sound. Not to mention two inlets and an ocean.

"Look, honey, hurry back to the station and see if you can catch Rosie before she gets off. You know where she keeps her launch?"

"With the wind where it is, she probably pulled up the creek beside the lifesaving station."

"Go. I'll start tracking."

"Tracking . . . I didn't think. The sand's still wet—Mac, can we—"

"Go!"

She went. And Mac set out, using the time-tested equipment that had been used by the first U.S. marshals more than two hundred years earlier—his eyes, his legs, and his common sense.

Between straggling tentacles of Bermuda grass, he found two clear sets of tracks to and from the back door. His and Banner's. Nothing under any of the windows but the deep trough made by rain sheeting off a steep roof. The front approach, however, offered a slightly different picture. Among several sets of tracks, most of them blurred and trampled, he identified his and Banner's. He'd used the front door once. She'd used it a couple of times, checking the condition of the road as the tide went down.

It was the most recent layer of tracks that riveted his attention. A service boot, short—about a man's size five— and a child's. That would be Rosie and the kid, but in what order?

It took less than two minutes for the picture to fall into place. First the park ranger had come up the front path and onto the porch. Then she'd come down the steps, looped around the side of the house, and sometime after that, the kid had come outside and headed in the opposite direction. Then the ranger had left.

Mac rounded the house, passing a disconnected fuel tank, several surprisingly well-groomed shrubs, a section of unpainted picket fence and the backside of the cistern. He'd seen the other end of the rectangular concrete structure when he'd dumped the oyster shells that morning.

Beyond the fence there was nothing but scrub. Water bushes, swamp willows, a few scrawny live oaks barely hanging on and a thicket of vine-covered cedars that had overgrown some sort of small building.

Garage? Net shed? Approaching it cautiously, Mac began to suspect it had been a precursor to indoor plumbing. When he saw the door hanging from a single rusted hinge, he was sure of it. He might not be an authority on architecture, but he'd be willing to bet this was a classic two-holer, complete with a crescent moon on the door.

"Ellie? Baby, let's go back home and have something to eat now. I brought you a treat you're not going to believe."

He listened, his narrowed eyes scanning the bush for a sign of movement. A few yards behind the ruined outhouse the high ground dropped off again. There could be a pond back there. Marsh was no safer—some of it looked dry enough to walk on, but it was riddled with creeks. A kid wouldn't be able to see over the bulrushes. She could wander for hours in that trackless wilderness, and even if she didn't stumble into a creek, once the sun went down and the temperatures started to fall . . .

"Ellie! Sweetheart, those pretty new shoes of yours are going to be mighty hard to clean up if you get 'em all muddy. I reckon we're going to have to buy you a pair of cowboy boots like mine if you're going to be out riding the range this way."

He waited. And watched.

And was rewarded. Two water bushes trembled. There was the sound of a tiny sneeze, and then a familiar red stocking cap poked through the brush.

Mac made himself wait until she came to him. There was wariness written all over her, along with the tracks of tears and a red, runny nose. She was clutching the battered monkey doll to her chest, and he'd been right about the shoes—her pink-and-white sneakers were not only dirty; they were wet.

I'm sorry.

It's okay, honey—everything's all right now that you're safe.

Am I going to be punished?

"Sweetheart, everything's all right. Let's go get you warm and dry, okay?" This time Mac spoke aloud, going on pure instinct. She was frightened of something. Of his anger? Maybe, but he had a hunch it was something more than that. Whatever had prompted her to run away, she'd come to him because she trusted him. And God help him, he would never give her cause to regret that trust.

"I hope you like strawberry ice cream, sprout. It's the only flavor they had."

By the time Banner had come back to report the little park service launch halfway out to the channel, Mac had peeled Ellie out of her wet shoes and socks and she was clumping around the kitchen in his boots while he heated a kettle of bathwater.

Banner did her best to hide her emotions, but by now he could read her like one of those old schoolbooks she valued so much. She was already attached to the kid. Dangerously attached.

The trouble was, so was Mac, and if anyone had a right to Tiffany Eleanore Keaton, he did. She was his niece, after all. She'd been handed over to him. In writing. Although legally speaking, neither of them had much of a claim, certainly nothing that would stand up in court against a determined third party.

While Ellie was soaking in a galvanized washtub full of warm water in the kitchen, Mac lay on the couch in the front parlor and smoked one of his three tattered cigarettes as he thought about the two women in his life.

In his life?

Yeah—in his life. For the moment, at least.

MacCasky had seen too much of the world in his thirty-eight years to believe in personal security. Still, he'd bought a measure of security for a five-year-old child. If there was something more to be gained, he would find it. Somehow he'd protect that child.

But as he lay there, watching smoke drift in a slow spiral toward the stark white ceiling in the barren room, it was not the child, but the woman who filled his thoughts.

* * *

Rosie the ranger had come through with canned chili, freeze-dried strawberry ice cream cubes, pork and beans and an overlooked stash of chocolate bars. Some ranger was going to be really ticked off come spring, when he looked in the file under *C*.

But best of all, there was half a jar of the finest powdered Colombian. Rich, dark, and loaded with caffeine!

Banner dressed the kid in her last clean outfit before lunch. And because Ellie was an enthusiastic trencherman, if not a particularly neat one, she wore a gingham napkin around her neck, cowboy-bandanna style. Along with the red stocking cap, she'd adopted that, and refused to give it up.

There was little conversation during their belated lunch. Banner limited the child to three cubes of the strawberry stuff and one bar of candy, and then supervised the brushing of her teeth.

Half an hour after the two of them disappeared up the stairs, Banner returned alone. "She's tucked into bed with her monkey. I told her I thought she needed a nap," she said to Mac, who lay sprawled on the iron-upholstered sofa. The smaller pieces of firewood she'd dragged out of the shed that morning had dried sufficiently to burn, and the room was comfortably warm.

Uncomfortably warm, in fact, Mac decided as he unbuttoned another button on his black flannel shirt.

"I'll shut off the damper," Banner offered as she came into the room. He watched as she manipulated the stack control and the lower door on the potbellied stove. "Don't get too warm—it's still cold as anything upstairs, and if you perspire now, you might chill later."

The look he sent her did not encourage coddling. He neither needed it nor wanted it.

"Mac, why did she run away? It's not like her to do that. At least I don't think it is," she added, frowning.

He didn't have the answer. There were a lot of answers he didn't have, and the questions were piling up faster than he could shove them under a rug. Three mugs of strong coffee after several days of tea had left him feeling edgy. That had to be the reason for his distraction. He had finally hung up his badge, and even though he was currently in the middle of investigating a case of child abandonment, at the moment even that seem irrelevant. All he could think of was that this was the last day he'd be spending with Banner Keaton.

It had to be the caffeine. It sure as hell couldn't be the nicotine—that last cigarette had tasted like the stuff she'd scrubbed off the oyster shells.

He was getting old; that was his trouble. The sooner he wound up this business and got on with his life, the better off he'd be.

And Banner...where would she be? Who would be with her, sharing her quiet observations, watching her move around a kitchen as a ballerina moved around a stage, bending, swaying, reaching out and up and over. Who would catch her smiles, see the glow in her eyes and share her thoughts, her laughter?

Who would hold her when she needed to cry, when she needed comfort—or when she just needed holding? Who would she turn to in the night when she burned for what only a lover could give her?

"I'm going out," he said, rising abruptly. He put on his boots, slipped one arm into his coat and then reached behind him, drawing out the small, flat gun. "I'm leaving this here with you. Put it somewhere out of sight, out of reach of the kid."

Banner's eyes widened, but she said nothing. She had known he had the thing, of course, but she'd tried to ignore it. What could she have said—throw it away? I've always hated guns?

She hadn't the right, and he would have refused.

"Take it, Banner," he said when she kept her hands behind her. "I don't think there's anything to worry about, but I'd feel better knowing you're able to protect yourself in case—"

"In case?" she whispered when he didn't go on.

"Look, I don't think the kid was playing. Something scared her into running. I don't know what it was, but I intend to take a look around while there's still some daylight left, and I'd just as soon not leave the two of you here unprotected. Lock up after me, and don't let anyone in until I get back, is that clear?"

"MacCasky, I've spent more time on this island than I can count, and I've never in my life locked a door. Well...maybe in the summertime. A few of the tourists seem to think everything on the island is open to the public. But even so, there's never been any real trouble."

"I'm not saying there's trouble now," he explained patiently. "All I'm saying is that the kid was—"

"Ellie."

His eyes narrowed, but then grudgingly he smiled. "All right. Ellie, then. She was scared stiff. I could see it on her face—I could almost hear it in her voice, only we both know she doesn't talk about whatever it is that's got her so locked up inside." The grudging smile was gone. His gray eyes were the exact color of an old seaman's grave marker she'd found as a child. And every bit as hard.

"There's no one else here. It's been too rough."

"Rosie made it."

"Until today, that is, but even so—"

"Look, I'm not saying the island's suddenly overrun with desperate fugitives, but I'd be a fool not to look around. Stay inside, stay awake and you'll be just fine. I'll be back before dark.''

He could tell she didn't like it, but finally she nodded. He laid the gun on the mantel, shoving it behind a yellowed photograph of a pair of hunters standing beside a small mountain of dead geese. Crossing to the front door, he turned and said, ''Remember to lock up after me.''

He had actually opened the door and stepped outside when he turned back. She was standing there, her hand on the knob, and without speaking, he caught her to him and bent his head to hers, capturing her mouth in a crushing kiss that went on and on until both of them were shaking. Mac was the first to draw away. He stared down at her, his angular cheeks flushed as if he'd been out in the wind too long.

Banner blinked twice in a dazed manner and then she lifted her eyes to his. As if she were waiting.

Waiting for what? For something he couldn't offer her?

Stepping back, Mac forced himself to release her. But he couldn't escape her eyes—those dark, disconcertingly direct eyes—so easily. It took an act of physical courage to turn away.

He knew she was watching him. Why didn't she go back inside?

Deliberately he raked a hand across his mouth, hoping she saw him—hoping she knew that he hadn't meant a damned thing by that kiss. It had been an impulse, that was all. A lousy impulse! What's more, he would tell her so, as soon as he took a look around.

No, he wouldn't tell her. Because it would be a lie. But he couldn't tell her that, either.

Ellie wasn't the only one who had problems communicating.

Nine

Ellie woke from her nap, and Banner fixed popcorn and weak hot tea and helped her cut up an old curtain and make a gown for her monkey.

Where had he gone? she wondered while the child played quietly with her stuffed toy. It didn't take all that long just to have a look around.

They cut paper dolls from old magazines, made a fancy convertible from a rice box and a bit of aluminum foil for them to ride around in, and after a while Banner heated more chili while Ellie set the table for three.

Just before dark the two of them gave up on waiting for Mac to return and ate supper.

There was no one else on the island. Mac was just being cautious, Banner assured herself. He'd probably taken a wrong turn and ended up all the way down in the Middle Village.

The third time she stepped out onto the porch to search the lengthening shadows for some sign of his return, she noticed that it had turned unexpectedly warm for January. But then, if there was one thing she'd learned about weather on the Outer Banks, it was to expect the unexpected.

She wasn't worried, really she wasn't. Mac had said he'd be back before dark, and technically speaking it wasn't even dark yet. A closer look at the sky revealed that at least a part of the darkness was caused by clouds. The wind seemed to be fitful, blowing from first this direction and then the other. Boxing the compass, Aunt Pearlie would have said. She'd had a saying to describe most everything.

And what would Aunt Pearlie have had to say about MacCasky Ford? That he was right smart of a man? That he was rough as a barnacle, hard as a hoe handle and too doggone fetching to be turned loose on any decent woman?

At a low rumble of distant thunder, Banner reluctantly stepped back inside and shut the door. Surely he knew enough to stay away from bogs. The island was full of natural hazards, but MacCasky was a grown man.

Deliberately forcing from her mind an image of just how fully grown the man was, she lighted a lamp in the front room and glanced inside the stove to see that the fire had burned itself out. And then, deliberately not looking at the mantel, where Mac's pistol was hidden, she marched back through the house to the kitchen.

He should have taken the thing with him. She didn't like guns. Never had. Besides, if he got into any trouble, he could have used it to signal with.

"We'll reheat Mac's supper when he gets here," she told the child calmly, just as if she weren't worried sick inside, wondering where he was, why he'd stayed away so long, what or whom he'd found—*what or who had found him*—trying in vain to assure herself that he was all right.

It was pitch-dark by the time she finally heard his step on the porch. She'd gone up to put Ellie to bed and stayed to have what Aunt Pearlie had always called a bird bath in the makeshift bathroom upstairs, changing into her last clean outfit, the one she'd saved to wear on the trip home.

And then, because the air inside was now considerably colder than that outside, she opened the windows and allowed the warm damp breezes to blow through.

That was when she heard him. Racing down the stairs, she met him at the front door, flinging it open before he could even touch the knob. Suddenly she was furious. Forgotten were all her fears that he'd been captured and hurt by some thug who'd come to the island for illicit purposes, or fallen into a pond, hit his head on a root and drowned. "Is this your idea of being back by dark?" she demanded.

"What the hell do you mean, opening the door like that? Dammit, woman, I ought to shake you good!"

She hung on to her temper by a shred, although she was quaking inside. "The next time you leave, don't bother to lie about when you'll be coming back."

"The next time I leave, I won't *be* coming back, God willing!"

"May I have that in writing?" It was all so horribly childish. Dimly she recognized that she was having a full-fledged temper tantrum, but at the moment she didn't seem to be able to help herself. She was thoroughly, even righteously, furious. It didn't help to know that if the anger collapsed, tears of relief would follow, and that would be the last straw. Try explaining tears to a hard case like MacCasky Ford.

"Are you going to let me inside?" He looked grim, angry and hot in the heavy sheepskin-lined coat. His face was flushed and his eyes were glacial, and Banner stepped back grudgingly and allowed him to come inside the house.

Not until he'd pushed past her and flung off his coat did she notice that he was wet up to his knees. Not only wet, but muddy. "Take off your boots, please, or I'll have to mop the floor again."

Without a word he dropped down onto the combination bench-coat-tree that had been a fixture in the hall for so long she scarcely even saw it anymore. One after the other he shucked off his muddy boots, and then he stood and unfastened his belt.

"I said your boots! What are you—"

"My jeans are muddy, too." Even as she stared, he loosened the belt and started in on the buttons on his fly, a look of malicious satisfaction on his face. "Lord knows, I wouldn't want you to have to mop any floors on my account."

"Mac, for goodness's sake, stop that!"

"For *goodness's* sake? It's been a long time since any woman appealed to my goodness, honey. I'm afraid you're broaching an empty cask."

Like a pillar of salt, she stood there, unable to move as he stepped out of his jeans and began unbuttoning his black flannel shirt. He wore an undershirt underneath, and it clung damply to his frame, hiding the multitude of scars but revealing his powerful muscles and hinting at the thatch of dark hair centered on his chest. It occurred to her that part of his condition might have to do with the fact that he was slightly overdressed for the sudden rise in temperature.

That didn't explain why she was suddenly too warm. "I'll get your bathrobe."

"I don't own a bathrobe."

"You know what I mean," she muttered as she hurried down the hall to his bedroom.

She was halfway there when lightning lit up the entire house. Moments later a blast of thunder rattled the windowpanes. She gasped, looked back to see him watching her and deliberately slowed her steps, just as if she hadn't been scared stiff of thunderstorms all her life.

MacCasky watched her disappear. In the back of his mind was the awareness that he was acting like a real bastard, but at the moment he was too tired to care.

He was back. She was safe. And he knew the kid was, too, or she'd have told him the minute she opened the door.

Sighing tiredly, he sprawled on the bench in his skivvies, wondering whether or not to tell her that someone had broken into a house about a quarter of a mile away by road—less than that as the crow flew. He'd walked from one side of the village to the other, from ocean to sound, checking out three docks and every creek that could be considered even marginally navigable. There was a small landing strip, but no sign that it had been used recently.

He'd walked around every house he'd been able to locate, but he might have missed a few. The deserted village wasn't exactly laid out in standard city-block fashion. Some thirty-odd buildings that he'd been able to count, a few little more than ruins, seemed to have been dropped in a random pattern on what little high ground existed on an island that was mostly marsh and shoreline.

Too tired to move, he watched her come back with the robe. She'd done something to her hair—it was twisted up into a coil on top of her head instead of being tied back with a shoestring. She was wearing something besides her usual flapping khaki layers, too. The black turtleneck sweater and tan flannel slacks covered her from feet to chin, but they were still a lot more revealing than anything he'd seen her in before.

And what they revealed didn't help what ailed him a damned bit. When he'd set out earlier in the day, he'd had one thing on his mind—to protect the kid. But somewhere along the line it was as if his mind had become possessed. Banner had been right there with him every muddy step of the way, past every lonesome little graveyard, every boarded-up house. In his mind he'd imagined he could hear her comments on everything. She could tease so quietly, with her dark eyes sparkling, that half the time he took her seriously.

Like a persistent little ghost, she'd followed him down paths that dwindled out to nothing, others that dead-ended in muddy creeks. She'd been right there grinning at him when he'd gone over his boot tops in what looked like an innocent patch of dried grass.

Mac had learned more than he ever wanted to know about voodoo and possession the last time he was in Haiti. He'd scoffed at the possibility and written it off as native superstition, but a few days with this woman just might make a believer out of him. Lord knows, she'd done *something* to him. Somehow she'd managed to work herself inside his head. If that constituted possession, then he was possessed.

Maybe things would get better if he could just reverse the process. Maybe if he possessed *her,* in the most basic sense of the word, he'd be cured.

Without a word she held out the robe, and he stood and turned his back, slipping both arms into the sleeves. If his ego had ever been in any danger of getting out of hand, it took only the thought of how he must look wearing a woman's striped flannel bathrobe and a pair of wet socks to trim it down to size.

While Banner reheated his supper, Mac headed for the upstairs bathroom—the one that had a tub, if no running water—and treated himself to a cold bath. Using the pitcher pump, he filled the bathtub half-full, helped himself to Banner's bar of fancy scented soap and lowered his naked body by painful degrees into the cold, tea-colored water.

She'd offered to heat some water in the kettle, but he'd declined. At the moment a cold bath was very much in order. He had to think, and the way that woman got under his skin, even when she was fighting him tooth and nail, he was having problems staying on track.

So she'd been worried about him. That was an interesting development. Oh, she would deny it if he accused her of it, but she'd been concerned, all right—otherwise, why had she jumped down his throat? It wasn't as if he'd spoiled a five-course dinner and disappointed a houseful of guests by showing up late for the party.

Okay, so she cared enough to worry about him when he ran a little late. He still owed her a good talking-to for opening the door without finding out who was on the other side.

He'd have to tell her about the break-in. He'd already made up his mind to stand guard tonight. By tomorrow they'd be out of here, and he wouldn't have to worry so much, but as long as they were here—as long as there was a possibility that some dirt-bag might be holed up here on the island with them—he couldn't afford to drop his guard.

Smothering a yawn, Mac ducked his head under the water, shook off the excess and then began working lather through his thick hair.

An hour later he watched her move around the kitchen. She was nice to watch. What harm could there be in just looking? "The kid give you any more trouble?" he asked over coffee—his third cup of genuine double strength un-decaffeinated instant coffee.

"None at all. I really wish I could communicate better with her, though. Why do you suppose she ran and hid like that? What could have frightened her, with the two of us right there in the house?"

"We were in the backyard, remember?" He stacked up his dishes and then forced himself to get up and take them to the sink.

"I'll do those," Banner offered.

"I made the mess. I'll clean it up." He pumped water into the dishpan and then added to it from the kettle. He'd been looking after himself since he was in grade school. He'd been brought up to believe that women were a luxury, not a necessity.

"I suppose you found the island crawling with danger-ous crooks. I hope they were impressed by your creden-tials, since you didn't have a badge or a gun to scare them off with."

Dense though he was on occasion, even MacCasky could recognize bravado when it came in the form of a husky, slightly unsteady denial. She was trying hard to be con-vincing. He took the blame himself—if he hadn't left her with the gun and warned her to lock up behind him, it would never have occurred to her to be frightened.

He regretted being the cause of her fear, but denying trouble wouldn't keep it away. Life wasn't that easy.

"I don't know about that, but it looks like someone might've broken into one of the houses. It's the next one across the marsh to the southeast, in sort of a flat place surrounded by big cedars. Looks like it's been shoved off its pins."

"The old dueling grounds, according to Aunt Pearlie. You wouldn't believe the stories she used to tell about what went on there. As for the house, I think it must have floated off the foundation during one of the hurricanes."

"That could do it, all right. I almost didn't see it through all those trees, but then I caught a glimpse of chimney and thought I'd better check it out. Damned good thing I did." He wasn't looking at her, but he could feel her tense up even before he heard the soft sound of a breath catching in her throat.

She didn't panic, though. Ten points for guts.

"You—went inside?"

"It was still boarded up pretty solid, and besides..." He shot her a smile, trying to ease those two small creases between her silky brows. "You had the gun, remember? I checked the outside, looked around for tracks. There's a concrete walk and a lot of rubble around on one side, but on the other, someone's been coming and going pretty regularly. Worn a track through the underbrush."

"How do you know someone's broken in, if it's all boarded up?"

"It can be arranged pretty easily. Whole boarded-up windows can be lifted out and put back in place, for that matter, but in this case it was something else. A corner of the screen on the back porch has been torn loose—several things knocked around there, although that could have been wind, I suppose."

"Or maybe not. Anything else?"

He turned to glance at her curiously, his hands dripping suds on the floor. "You're pretty cool about this, considering you were ready to take my head off a little while ago."

He watched the color rise to her face, and it was all he could do not to grin like a possum. For all her coolness under fire, this was one warm-blooded lady. One sweet, laid-back, hot-tempered, warmhearted lady. "Yeah, matter of fact, what caught my eye first was a hole in the roof right next to the chimney, just big enough for a man to slip through. Which means that, unless we're dealing with Santa's elves here, someone's built himself a handy little skylight. Nine times out of ten it would never be noticed, but I happened to be watching a pair of big white birds fly over, and it caught my eye.''

Banner moved behind him on her way to the stove. When she brushed against him, Mac caught his breath and tightened his grip on a fistful of silverware until he had himself back under control. If that was all it took—the brush of her body against his and that warm, womanly scent that clung to her skin, then he was in even worse shape than he'd suspected.

She lifted the kettle, questioning him with a lift of an eyebrow, and he shook his head. ''Nah, I'd better not,'' he said as soon as he could trust his voice. ''I'll be drinking coffee all night, as it is, and there's not that much left in the jar.''

''All night? You're out on your feet, Mac. I'm amazed you've lasted this long.''

''Surprising what hot food and a cold bath can do to revive a man, hmm?'' He could think of something he wanted a hell of a lot more than he wanted another cup of coffee, but he didn't think she was ready to hear about that. ''I'm good for the rest of the night, but I'd better save the coffee for later, thanks.''

''Look, if you've got some misguided notion about staying awake to protect Ellie, then forget it. I've got at least another hour of packing up to do, and then I've got to mop up here in the kitchen and sweep out the front rooms. You go on to bed. If someone tries to break in, I promise you, I'll yell my head off.''

''Forget it, honey—I'm wide-awake. Couldn't sleep now if I tried.'' And then he spoiled the effect by yawning.

Banner laughed. Coming up behind him, she put both hands playfully on his back and gave him a push in the direction of the door, but her hands slipped on the loose-fitting bathrobe and slid along his sides. Swearing softly under his breath, Mac grabbed her by both wrists before she could react, drawing her arms the rest of the way around him to hold her tightly against his back.

"Mac, you're wasting good sleeping time," she said with a laugh that sounded strangely constricted.

He could feel her cheek resting against his shoulder, her breasts pressed against his back and her soft belly pushing into his backside. Fires that had ignited the first time he'd seen her, when he'd gathered her up in his arms—fires he had hoped were quenched by the cold bath he'd taken earlier—now threatened to blaze up out of control.

"Go to bed, Banner," he ordered gruffly. "You can get up early in the morning and do your packing and cleaning." But he was still holding her hands so that her arms were wrapped tightly around his middle. It felt so good he would have welded her there if he could have got away with it.

A blast of thunder rocked the house, causing her to tighten her grip. "Not scared of a little lightning, are you?" he teased.

He was scared. He was shaking all over, and it had nothing to do with the unseasonal thunderstorm. "Go to bed, will you?" he growled, still not releasing her.

"The mopping—I might not have time tomorrow...."

"Rosie'll forgive you."

"But Aunt Pearlie wouldn't," she said breathlessly.

And then the rain started, and she tried to pull away. "The windows—upstairs. I left them open."

An alarm went off in his mind, and Mac slammed down on it, silencing it ruthlessly. It was too late for warnings. It had probably been too late the minute he'd turned the

Blazer four-by-four south on Highway 168 and headed for the Outer Banks.

"I'll help you," he said, and wondered with grim amusement if he was going to see his life flashing before his eyes before he could make it up the stairs.

They did Ellie's room first. The child slept soundly, her monkey in its kitchen-curtain nightgown hanging by his tail from one small fist. Next they did the front window that overlooked the stairs. "I'll do mine," Banner said, her voice little more than a whisper.

The inference was that he should go back downstairs and do his own. Mac rejected it. Just as he rejected all the warning bulletins his subconscious was issuing. "Mine's on the off side. It's raining from the other direction."

He followed her into her bedroom, and before either of them could cross to the double windows, he caught her hand and swung her around to face him. "Banner, I want to make love to you. If you don't want it, then tell me right now, because after that it will be too late."

She stared at him, her face only dimly visible in the light from the hall. Her eyes looked enormous, and he thought her lips were trembling. It was all the invitation he needed.

In a single moment Banner went from being a mature, sensible woman to being a wild, irresponsible creature conscious only of her own burgeoning needs. Time, place and reality disappeared in a flash of lightning. The only reality was Mac's arms holding her against his aroused body, his mouth touching hers, lifting and then coming back from a different angle to move sensitively over the contours of her face.

He didn't try to deepen the kiss—not at first. His hands on her back were warm and hard as he moved them up to her shoulders and into her hair, destroying its neat order.

They slipped down over her hips, his strong fingers kneading her flesh, holding her against him so that she could be in no doubt of his own fierce hunger. In contrast to the urgency of his body, his mouth continued to brush slowly back and forth over hers, demanding nothing, yet compelling all she had to give. She could feel the ragged thunder of his heart echoed in her own pulses. For endless moments his kiss remained a tenuous thing, as if he were intent on memorizing every curve, every swell, each small indentation of her lips.

It was Banner who broke first. She opened her mouth under his, and Mac groaned deep in his throat and moved with her the few short steps to the bed. Bearing her down under his body, he kissed her as though he were starving for the taste of her, the feel of her mouth under his, her breast under his hands—her slight frame under his powerfully aroused one.

He explored her mouth as he explored her body, slowly and with trembling sensitivity. Now and then he would break away, burying his face in her throat as his breath rasped hotly against her skin.

"Banner—sweet heaven, woman, I'm not sure I can handle this!"

Banner wasn't sure, either. All she knew was that if he left her now, she would die. None of this made sense. She would probably regret it later, but for now all she could think of was what MacCasky was offering her. Relief. Release. But more than that—for a little while at least, she could pretend that he loved her, too.

"I—wait a minute, love," he rasped, and before she could hold him, he was gone, leaving her feeling cold, empty, lost. *Wait for what? I've waited all my life. After tonight I'll be left waiting again, but at least give me this much.*

"Mac?" she called out softly just as he reappeared. He'd removed the bathrobe. Silhouetted against the lamplight, his broad-shouldered body with the lean flanks, the long, powerful legs, looked almost threatening.

"I had something in my shaving kit," he said, and as if he'd felt the sudden chill of disappointment that stole over her, he added, "It's been there for a long time, Banner. I didn't bring it along on the off chance, and I'm not promiscuous by nature, in spite of the way this looks."

She held out a hand and he sat down beside her, lifting her up to peel the turtleneck sweater over her head. "I never said—"

"You probably thought it. I wouldn't blame you, but sweetheart, I want you to understand this. It's you. It's not the circumstances or the fact that it's been a long time for me—it's you. The first time I laid eyes on you, I felt like I'd been punched out. Then, when I picked you up off the floor..."

"I know," she whispered, trying hard not to allow her joy to burn too brightly. He'd felt it, too. She wasn't alone, then. This wasn't just a one-sided infatuation. A matter of chemistry or biology. "Mac, I feel the same way."

It took far less time for them to remove the last of their clothing than it had to put it on. When there was nothing left between them, he came down beside her again.

Mac knew something about explosives—he'd never experienced anything as incendiary as the touch of her naked body against his. Something told him that even if they'd both been dressed in solid asbestos, it wouldn't have mattered. No fire wall on earth could have withstood what was happening to them.

More shaken than he cared to admit, he took her face between his two hands and stared down into her eyes. "You're very special to me, Banner Keaton," he said deeply, softly.

And then he kissed her, slowly and thoroughly. When she was all but helpless with need, he moved over her, parting her thighs to kneel between them. Slowly he brought his mouth down from her lips to her breast, leaving behind a trail of sheer sensation. His lips closed over her sensitive nipple, and she dug her head back into the pillow and shifted her legs restlessly as course after course of lightning pierced her body.

"Please, oh please, oh please," she was whispering without even knowing she'd spoken aloud. He was fondling the delicate angle of her hipbone, and his hand slipped into the hollow of her abdomen. When she felt his tongue begin to circle her navel, she gasped and drew up her knees, pressing his head into her soft flesh.

Her eyes widened in the darkness, and she uttered a soft whimper as he found her. Endless moments later, shuddering uncontrollably, she drew him up over her body, wordlessly pleading with him to fill the emptiness inside her—to fill her and make her whole again.

At the last moment he hesitated. She could feel him hot and hard, moving against her. "Tell me again, Banner—tell me you want this. I need to be sure you want it as much as I do."

"Please, Mac—I'll die if you don't make love to me now," she said simply.

And he did. Fiercely at first, and then more slowly, as if he were pacing himself, trying to sustain the sweet torment as long as possible.

But it had gone on too long. She needed him desperately, and she needed him now. Thrusting against his slow stroke, she raked her hands through his hair, bringing his head down so that she could kiss him again and again. And then together, gasping, kissing, racing the tide even as it broke over their heads, they shouted softly and they whispered, speaking words that had no meaning outside that single moment in time.

At least that's what Banner tried to tell herself later, when she lay sated, exhausted and damp, still entangled in Mac's strong arms.

She didn't love him. Not really. She couldn't have fallen in love so quickly. It just didn't happen that way.

Oh, no? And how long did it take you to fall in love with Rory?

A matter of hours, and look how that ended!

But Mac's a different man. And you're a different woman now.

I can't *love him. I* don't *love him!*

But she could and she did. What's more, she was very much afraid she'd blurted out her feelings, which left her with nothing at all—not even her pride.

Astride a tilted kitchen chair an hour later, Mac smoked his last cigarette and stared out the window at the fast-moving clouds. A moon had risen—just a sliver, but it was enough to make the shadows come alive.

He'd done some stupid things in his life, but none to compare with what had just happened. He'd waited until she was asleep, drawn the covers up over her and opened the window. The rain had ended by then. For a long time he'd stood there gazing down at her sleeping face, wondering why one face out of ten thousand—out of a hundred thousand—should affect him the way hers did.

She'd said she loved him. He had to believe she didn't mean it. Women said things in the heat of the moment—men did, too, but he'd never told a woman he loved her. Nor had he told Banner that.

All the same, somehow he had to let her know that it couldn't happen again. She was special. She would always be special to him, but just as he'd told himself about the kid, she needed someone who could love her back, someone who would be around tomorrow and all the tomorrows after that.

And MacCasky was not that man. Some men were cut out for the long haul—some weren't. He'd been a loner for too many years to think he could change now, no matter how much he might want to.

Ten

The morning went fast, but there had been time to think during the slow hours of the night. Too much time MacCasky knew now as he watched Banner move from room to room, checking each window to see that the blinds were hooked properly and the sashes securely locked.

She wore the black-and-tan outfit, with flat-heeled boots and a cinnamon suede jacket that came close to matching her hair. They'd spoken little this morning outside the necessary, but he hadn't missed the quick shy glances she'd sent his way when she thought he wasn't looking.

He'd screwed up again. The last time he'd messed up a mission so badly it had been because he'd gone back in to rescue a couple of stupid tourists who should have had better sense than to go exploring a country whose governments rose and fell with monotonous regularity, where lawlessness and corruption were a way of life.

This time he'd screwed up on account of the way a particular woman moved, the way she looked. The way she smelled.

This time there was no Julio. There were no White Doves, no *Hombres Nieves,* no local turf wars—just a man, a child and a woman.

And he'd blown it again.

Banner stopped by the bathroom door where he was opening drains to ask if he'd checked upstairs.

"Yeah—it's all clear. Windows locked, blinds shut, all baggage accounted for. What about down here? Think the kid wants to use the facility one last time before we take off?"

She shook her head. "We're all finished and ready to head for the dock." Mac had already carted all her boxes to the wharf, stacking them three high on the cart and making two trips.

"I'll catch up with you, then," he said, needing a few more minutes alone to get his head together.

He heard her hesitate, heard her light footsteps moving away, and he sighed. All the time in the world wasn't going to get him out of this one. He'd known before he'd ever left her bed the night before that nothing was ever going to be the same. In less than a week she had turned his whole world upside down, changing the way he thought, the way he reacted—hell, even the way he breathed!

Last night had been so special it scared him to think about it. It had never before happened like that for him—the feeling that he'd died and been reborn as part of another person. He'd known pleasure, sure. That's what it was all about.

But last night had been something more than mere pleasure. He didn't know what it was—there weren't any words to describe it, but whatever it was, he knew it would never happen to him again.

What was infinitely worse, he knew that within that small space of time when he'd held her in his arms and joined his body with hers, his entire life had been irreversibly changed.

Captain Julius was prompt. Mac loaded the freight aboard first and helped the old man stow it. Then he handed Banner down, not allowing his hand to linger on hers. Not allowing himself to meet her eyes.

"Ready to go, sprout? We've had us one helluva—"

"Mac," Banner said softly, reproof and laughter in her voice.

"—one heckuva vacation, haven't we? The accommodations might not be much to brag about, but the staff was first-class, huh? Now...what would you say to a big cheeseburger and fries for lunch?"

He swung her into Banner's waiting arms, cast off the lines and leapt aboard, taking his place beside the captain. Nor did he look back, not at the woman and child on the padded locker behind him—not at the island itself.

Mac told himself it wasn't because he was afraid to look back. Then he told himself he was lying. And then he told himself it was a damned good thing he'd retired when he had—he was definitely losing his grip!

The trip back to Ocracoke seemed to take only a fraction of the time the outward journey had taken. Once at the dock, Banner dug out her billfold to pay her own fare, but Mac waved her away.

She didn't argue. "Come on, Ellie, we'll go over to the ferry terminal and wash up before we head home, shall we?"

Mac glanced over his shoulder. "Run along, I'll catch up with you in a minute. I want to have a word with the captain."

He wanted to see if the man had ferried another passenger over to the island within the past week, but it seemed he hadn't. Nor did he know of anyone else who had.

Banner and Ellie were coming out of the ferry terminal when the little girl gasped softly and grabbed Banner's leg.

"Ellie? What's wrong, honey?"

There was no answer, of course. What had she expected? Kneeling, Banner held the rigid figure away from her and tried to read her face. It wasn't hard to do. What came through was pure, unreasoning fear.

Glancing over her shoulder, she tried to see what could have terrorized the child who, only a moment before, had been skipping along at her side, swinging her monkey by the tail.

There was nothing to see. Just a truck parked across the street, but it was empty. A dog had sidled up to the flagpole to lift his leg, and a man wearing the uniform of a park ranger went into a store across the way.

"Is that it, darling? You're afraid of dogs?"

Small arms pulled her closer with surprising strength, and Ellie buried her face on Banner's shoulder. "But honey, he's not going to hurt you. See? He's already done his business and gone. He probably belongs to that little boy who just rode by on a bicycle."

The arms tightened. "Ellie, talk to me. I know you can talk, darling, because I've heard you. Now tell me what's bothering you, and I promise I'll take care of it. I won't let anything hurt you, don't you know that? I love you, Ellie, and when people love each other, they take care of each other."

"Why don't you two head for the Hatteras Inlet ferry? I want to speak to the ranger about—uh, an open house over on Portsmouth." Mac had come up quietly behind them, and he gave her a meaningful look.

Banner nodded. "Good idea. He could call down to Cape Lookout headquarters and have someone check it out," she said quietly.

Mac swung Ellie up into his arms, seating her on his shoulder. "Up we go, kid. I'm warning you, though—if that monkey of yours bites me on the back, I'm cutting his banana ration."

Banner stared after the two of them, wondering how she was going to be able to stand losing the child. Or the man. Not that she'd ever had either one of them—only temporary custody. She hurried to catch up with them. "We'll look for restaurants along the way. Ellie can help watch, can't you, darling?"

The timing was perfect. Mac's Blazer four-by-four caught up with Banner's station wagon about a mile from the inlet. A ferry had just unloaded when they reached the northern tip of Ocracoke, and was getting ready to pull out again. They drove directly aboard, directed by the attendant to opposite sides of the bargelike craft.

Banner had expected Mac to join them in her car, but he remained in his own. They were in plain view of each other, but not once did he even look their way. Determined to ignore the small hurt she felt, Banner directed Ellie's attention to whatever sights presented themselves in the middle of Hatteras Inlet. A flock of gulls. A cormorant perched on a channel marker. A small fishing boat.

Only when she couldn't help herself did she glance across at the dark blue Blazer four-by-four. They might as well have been strangers, she thought, hurt and confused. Arms crossed over his chest, Mac seemed to be sleeping.

Well, it's no wonder, she thought guiltily. He'd stayed awake all night long guarding them after he'd left her bed.

That had been a major mistake. One she was going to have to try very hard to forget. From the looks of him, she thought after a quick sidelong glance, he'd had no trouble forgetting.

While Ellie poked tiny curious fingers under the flaps of the boxes stacked in the back seat, Banner fought off a feeling of depression that threatened to swamp her. After she'd lost her baby, she had sunk so low she couldn't get through a single day without crying her heart out.

She'd been that route. She had no more time or energy to waste on tears. Certainly not for a man she had known less than a week—a man she'd slept with once. A man who had let her know by word, deed and gesture right from the first that commitment was not a part of his life-style.

She wasn't any more interested in commitment than he was. Even if he'd asked her—which he hadn't—she would have turned him down.

Sure you would. If you were crawling on your belly across the Sahara Desert, you'd turn down a glass of ice water, too.

MacCasky crossed his arms behind his head and closed his eyes as the sturdy little ferry plowed through the turbulent waters of the inlet, headed for a rendezvous with Hatteras Island. He told himself it was an excellent opportunity to catch up on his sleep.

The trouble was, he had too much on his mind. Too much eating a hole in his gut. The last thing he needed on top of everything else was an ulcer, but if he didn't wind this thing up PDQ and head for the hills, he'd be having his antacids freighted in by the truckload.

He knew exactly where he'd fouled up. Mistake number one had been hanging around. He should have settled things quickly with the woman and got the hell off the island. It had been a bad lead. He should never have got himself involved.

Mistake number two had been letting Banner get too attached to the kid. Because she was, and he knew it. And every step he took to find the real mother brought him that much closer to dealing her the kind of pain no woman deserved.

Mistake number three had been making love to her. Not just having sex—at thirty-eight he knew the difference between making love and having sex. At least he did now. Before last night he'd have sworn it was all a matter of semantics.

He wasn't running away, Mac told himself—he was doing what he had to do. Once an agent, always an agent. He'd spent the better part of his life tracking down fugitives of one kind or another.

He almost wished that this time he wouldn't succeed. If he couldn't find the mother, then who was to say he couldn't keep the kid himself? And if Ellie was his, and he decided she'd be better off with Banner, then who could object? They needed each other. And the last thing he needed was a five-year-old dependent.

But he was good. He would find his answers, one way or another. He always did. He would tackle Harrison Keaton, get a lead on the mother, find her and haul her off to a lawyer and make this thing all nice and legal. He'd go through whatever channels he had to, but Banner was going to end up with that little girl if he had to break a few heads to arrange it! Or a few rules.

And then he would leave them alone. He'd arrange financial support—hell, he didn't have anyone else to help him spend his money—and then he'd get out of their lives. It was better all around that way.

They found a restaurant on Hatteras that was still open in the off-season and had lunch. Standing outside afterward, they exchanged phone numbers and addresses. At least, Banner gave him hers. He didn't even know his new one yet. Rural route something-or-other, Wilkes County, probably. He gave her Conner's number in Norfolk and told her she could always reach him through the office.

And then he surprised the hell out of himself by saying, "Look, why don't I just follow you on home and check things out—see that you're settled in all right before I take off again?"

"That's really not necessary, but thanks," she said politely, just as if she hadn't come apart in his arms twelve hours before.

"Hey, no problem. It's practically on the way. I'd feel better, checking the place over—not that I'm looking for trouble, but it doesn't pay to be careless."

"That reminds me, what did the ranger say when you told him about the...you know." She glanced down at Ellie, who was picking up bits of river rock from the parking lot and putting them into her pockets.

"Said he'd let the other team know. I think he thought I was paranoid."

"Didn't you tell him who you were?"

"And have him wonder what I was doing, following you over there in the first place?"

She stared at the winter-bleak waterfront across the highway. "Oh. I suppose you're right."

Mac's hand came up as he reached out to her, and then it fell to his side. "Better get going. It's what—a four-hour ride?"

"Three, this time of year. Mac, honestly, you don't have to go with us. We'll be all right."

"Let's get on with it, shall we? Come on, honey—" He waved Ellie over, and she trotted obediently to his side. "Time to go."

When he saw how very low the child sat—not even tall enough to see through the windshield—he removed his thick coat and folded it into a cushion. Lifting her on top of it, he fastened her seat belt securely, grinned and yanked on her ponytail. "If you wanna stop or anything, reach out and pinch the driver, you hear? I want that coat back in first-class condition."

Later he tried to blame Ellie's impish grin for throwing him off balance. Banner was already at her door when he came around to her side of the car. His hand closed over hers on the door latch, and then his eyes caught hers and he lost it completely.

"Ah, honey, why did it have to be you?" he said with a soft groan, and before either of them could think better of it, he caught her to him and kissed her until the rest of the world disappeared.

They stopped for gas somewhere in Currituck County. Mac could have made it to Norfolk easily, as he had an auxiliary tank, but Banner's miniwagon was running on fumes.

"It's not too late to change your mind," she reminded him just before they left the service station. "One-sixty-eight north turns off just up ahead."

"Forget it. I need to see where Ellie'll be staying. She's my only relative, after all." A wintery smile lit his gray eyes, and Banner felt her knees weaken.

She made a deliberate effort to get a hold of herself. Just because last night he'd taught her things about her own body she'd never even dreamed of before, just because a couple of hours ago he'd kissed her until she could barely stand up, that didn't mean a thing. Nothing had changed. A kiss was not a promise. "Well," she said after clearing her throat. "You do understand that I'll only be in Elizabeth City for as long as it takes to get Aunt Pearlie's house ready to turn over to the realtor. After that I'll be going back to my apartment in Murfreesboro. There's a cot in my studio that Ellie can have. And there's a playground not far away. It's really a beautiful little town...."

"You don't have to sell me, Banner." His voice was flat, but he was staring at her mouth so hard she began nibbling on her lip.

"There's plenty of room. And—and a nice yard. I'm sure I'll be able to find someone dependable to keep her when I'm in class. You don't have to worry about that."

"Let's move out, okay? I plan to be on the way north by dark."

But plans had a way of not working out, as Mac discovered later. The first thing that happened was meeting Banner's next-door neighbor, a highway patrolman, who was just coming off duty.

Ellie went catatonic. Her eyes wide with fright in her white face, she gripped Mac's coat and refused to leave the car. At first neither of them caught the significance, but when Officer Williams sauntered over to the car to tell Banner that there were a couple of mail deliveries in his kitchen for her, there could be no mistaking the focus of the child's unreasoning fear.

"I di'n't mean to do it, I di'n't mean to do it," she whimpered.

Stunned, the three adults stared at the tiny figure. Mac broke first. "Officer, would you mind moving off? For some reason the kid's afraid of uniforms." Now that he saw it, it was perfectly obvious. Uniforms. It wasn't the man—just as it hadn't been Rosie. It was the uniform. Anyone in uniform, evidently, had the same effect.

By the time they got her inside, Ellie had stopped whimpering, although it took both of them to pry her fingers out of Banner's sweater.

"Go make some cocoa or something sweet and hot," Mac said under his breath. "I'll take over here for now."

"Are you sure? Maybe she needs a woman."

"Go."

It was several hours later before they were able to get the child to sleep. Only then did they sit down and begin to piece together the bits and pieces. Ellie still wasn't talking freely, but they'd been able to get enough out of her by holding, soothing and even rocking her in Pearlie's spraddle-armed old wicker rocker, to put together a picture of what must have happened.

It was chilling in its simplicity. Nothing overtly cruel—nothing that could really be called child abuse, yet it had had a profound effect on a fatherless five-year-old.

Even now, Banner couldn't think of it without wanting to cry.

To recover her composure, she offered to fix Mac a sandwich. They'd made scrambled eggs and toast for Ellie before putting her to bed in Banner's bed, with her monkey clutched in her arms and Terrence, Aunt Pearlie's big yellow tomcat, who'd been cared for by the Williamses next door, at her feet.

"Yeah, I could go for that. Anything will do—how about a bacon-and-egg sandwich?"

Relieved to have something to occupy a fraction of her mind for a few minutes, Banner headed for the kitchen.

Mac was right behind her. She opened the refrigerator, took out the eggs again and when she turned, she bumped into him. He caught the eggs, placed them on the table and took her by the shoulders. "Are you all right, honey?"

"I will be. I mean, of course I am. It just makes me furious to think of frightening a child that way. No wonder the poor little darling never said anything. Can you imagine any mother threatening her own child with the police?"

"A mother who'd go off and leave a five-year-old alone all day and half the night or more? Yeah, I can imagine it." What his own mother had done paled in comparison. At least he'd never been neglected while she was living with them.

"But to have threatened her by saying if she told anyone about being all alone in the house, the policemen would come and take her away and she'd never see her mother again! Oh, I could cry!"

Later Banner would tell herself it was because she'd been too tired and too emotional to think straight. They were both feeling raw, needing comfort, and it was too easy to let herself take that one small step that would bring her into Mac's arms.

Did she take it, or did he? Banner never knew, but either way the results were the same.

Explosive.

Mac lowered his face to hers, rubbing his beard-roughened cheek against her hair and against her own smooth cheek, and then angling his mouth over hers. Between kisses—tender ones, hungry ones, soft brushing kisses and urgent, plunging kisses—he whispered broken words of need. She drank them in thirstily and whispered of love, helpless to hold back.

Eventually he led her back into the living room, onto the neatly spread daybed, where Banner planned to sleep that night. No more words were spoken as he quickly removed first her clothes and then his own. With infinite tenderness she touched the scar on his shoulder, first with her fingertips, then with her lips. And then her lips trailed down his chest, kissing, tasting—burrowing into his hard, resilient flesh.

"You're so beautiful," he said with a groan, holding her up over him so that his gaze could roam down over her body. "I never knew how beautiful a woman could be."

He ignored her shy denial. She was perfect in his eyes—small, compactly built, flaring sweetly where a woman should flare, curving in at the waist, swelling out at the breast. Hungrily he gazed down over the soft, barely perceptible slope of her belly to the feathering of russet curls below.

Perfect. It didn't occur to him that he'd never even seen her in a dress, much less a lacy nightgown. All he knew was that she was the most gloriously feminine creature he had ever beheld.

Slowly he brought her forward so that he could take the rose-brown tip of her breast between his lips, and then it was Banner's turn to groan. By the time he lifted his head to smile at her, he was barely able to hang on to his control. "You like that, hmm?"

Their heated breath mingled, their voices were barely audible and both were trembling hard. "Oh, yesss," Banner whispered. With unsteady hands Mac spread her legs, turning her so that she was kneeling astride his lap. He lowered her onto himself with such exquisite slowness that she moaned softly, curling over to bury the sound in his throat.

For a moment she moved frantically, as though startled at finding herself in such a position. Then he began thrusting against her, unable to wait, and her eyes widened. Sweat beaded her flushed face, and even as Mac watched, she began to tighten around him. He urged her on with short, hard strokes, pressing her hard against him.

It was the most beautiful thing he had ever witnessed. And then, while she still trembled tightly around him, he thrust twice more and shuddered as he was ripped apart by his own fire storm.

They lay woven together, dozing, waking, moving little, until finally his cooling body reminded MacCasky that it was time to go.

"Oh, can't you stay?"

"I'd better get on with it. The sooner we get this mess settled, the better I like it." More shaken than he dared admit, he sat on the side of the bed and looked around for his clothes.

"Did someone scratch your back with a hay rake?" Her palm smoothed over the scars on his lower back, and he stiffened and then relaxed.

It was the second time she'd mentioned his scars, although he'd seen the look in her eyes the first time she'd seen him without his shirt. She'd been shocked, but not repulsed. "Yeah, that's about what happened. No more sleeping in haystacks for me."

She let it go, but he could tell she wasn't satisfied with the answer. Reaching for his clothes, he headed for the bathroom. He needed time—he needed space. Things were happening too damned fast.

The phone rang, and he paused in the doorway while she answered it. It occurred to him for the first time that she had a whole life that didn't include him, and suddenly he found himself resenting it.

"Oh, Mrs. Williams," she said, and Mac slotted the name into a mental file labeled Neighbor.

"No, tomorrow will be soon enough, but thank you. And thanks for looking after Terrence. Good night."

"Checking up on you?" Mac asked.

"No, of course not. Why don't I go make coffee while you get dressed?"

He had to hand it to her. Little things like a whisker burn on her throat, her lips swollen from his kisses, and the fact that she'd just come apart in his arms didn't faze her for a minute. The lady was cool, all right. Too damned cool! She recovered fast, but he happened to know she wasn't quite as unflappable as she pretended.

Mac took his coffee black and on his feet. Pacing the small room, he tried to ignore her, but it was like steel trying to ignore a magnet.

"More coffee?" she asked graciously. She'd dressed quickly and done something to her hair. The high neck of her sweater now hid his whisker burn, and perversely he wanted to fold it back so that the whole world could see his brand on her skin. If that made him a chauvinistic bastard, so be it.

"Ten-twenty. I'd better hit the road," he said, placing his mug on a lace-covered stand beside an overgrown fern.

"Don't worry about Ellie, Mac, I'll take good care of her."

"Yeah, I know that." He was having trouble meeting her eyes, his conscience bothering him on more than one count. "Banner, try not to care too much, huh? At least not until I get this business sorted out."

He couldn't make her any promises. There were at least two other people who had a stronger claim on the kid than he did, and even if he managed to work his way through that, there were certain inescapable legalities. Out on a deserted barrier island, he'd been able to rationalize putting those two together because they so obviously needed each other—they were right for each other. But they were back in the real world now. He couldn't guarantee anything.

Banner's smile was a bit too brittle, her eyes too bright to be convincing. "You're a little late with your advice."

It wasn't the pain in his shoulder that caused him to wince as he shrugged into his coat. "I know, honey. All I can say is, I'll do my best. You're not in this alone, you know."

Did that mean he cared for her? Or that he, too, cared for the child? After he left, Banner stared at the door as if will alone could bring him back.

Eleven

———

There was disillusionment in Harrison Keaton's faded eyes, a bitter twist to his thin lips. Unexpectedly Mac-Casky found himself feeling sorry for the old man he had tracked to a luxurious nursing home.

"Then you don't know where she is?" he asked.

"The Cargin woman? No. Not interested in where she is. I told her before when she tried to get money out of me that if I had to pay off every little tramp my son bedded, I'd be a poor man."

"But what about your granddaughter?"

"Humph! That what she tell you?"

Patiently Mac reminded the old man that he had never met the woman in person. Carol Jewel Cargin hadn't hung around long enough to be thanked, nor had she seen fit to sign her letter. "She claims Ellie's your granddaughter, Colonel Keaton." Mac had tried to hang on to his hatred of the man who had robbed him of his own mother, but pity had leached it away. The old soldier was completely alone now, from all reports. His body was a wreck. At this point Mac wasn't altogether sure about his mind.

A bleak smile flickered across his face as he considered the fact that they might be two of a kind in that respect. "Colonel?"

"Wha—Oh. You still here?"

"What about the little girl? Any chance she could be your granddaughter? Could your son and this Cargin woman have been married? She claims the kid's named Tiffany Eleanore Keaton."

"How the dickens do I know if he married her? The boy never listened to anything I had to say. He had no right to use Eleanore's name for one of his bastards!"

"Legitimate or not, she could still be your grandchild, sir."

But Harrison Keaton was off on another tangent. "My boy already had himself a wife. Redheaded woman—not much to say for herself. Told him *that* was a mistake, too, but would he listen? Why didn't *she* give him a child if he was so hell bent on having one?"

"I wouldn't know, Colonel Keaton. I don't even know that the child is his, but Banner—that's the woman your son married—"

"Your half brother," the man in the wheelchair cut in.

"All right, my half brother— Anyhow, Rory's ex-wife says the child has his eyes. She'd be in a position to know, wouldn't she? I seriously doubt that she'd make a mistake about something like that—not under the circumstances."

Harrison Keaton was silent for so long, Mac thought he'd dozed off again. The nurse had warned him that he did this frequently, and that his attention span wasn't what it used to be.

"Hurt you bad, didn't she?" he said, catching Mac off guard.

"Banner?"

"No, not Banner," the old man dismissed with a snort of disgust. "Eleanore! My Ellie."

This was why Mac hadn't wanted to come in the first place, but Conner had insisted he couldn't spare anyone. Besides, it was Mac's business, and if he wanted it to remain unofficial, he was going to have to cover all bases personally. "I was seven years old then, sir. I don't remember a whole lot about it."

"No, not much you don't," the old man retorted with a wicked chuckle. "She was mine before she was yours, sonny—don't you forget that. If I hadn't got on my high horse, she'd never have married Ford, and you wouldn't even be here. But Ellie and I, we had words and I went off to Korea, and when I came back it was too late. She'd married that—that damned carpenter!"

It all came flooding back then—all the hurt, all the rage he had felt and not been able to express as a child. "That carpenter, as you call him, was my father. Eleanore Ford had made her choice. Why the hell couldn't you have let her alone?" Mac demanded before he could stop himself. This sick old man was no match for him. Besides, it was all water under the bridge.

As if he hadn't heard a word, Harrison Keaton continued to speak, his rheumy eyes on a distant past that MacCasky wanted no part of. "I married, too—did she tell you? Pride, boy. Pride can be a terrible thing when it's used as a weapon. Ruth was a good woman, better than I ever deserved, God rest her soul. When she died, I resigned my commission and wrote to Ellie."

Ellie, his mother. Not Ellie the little girl. Mac felt a desperate need to regain control of the conversation. "The child, Colonel Keaton—I need to locate her mother. Can you think of anything that—''

''She never really got over it, you know. It hurt her to leave you, but it was her own choice.''

MacCasky stood and reached for his coat. He'd had enough. There was no help to be found here—the old veteran was too far gone. He probably wouldn't have helped even if he'd known anything.

''—couldn't just go off and take everything that poor devil had. You were what she loved most, boy—so you were what she left behind.''

Mac didn't want to hear any of this. What good did it do now? It was nearly thirty years too late. ''I appreciate your time, Colonel Keaton.''

''What's she like, boy?''

The question halted him halfway to the door of the solarium. ''Who, my mother? The kid's mother?''

''My granddaughter. Little Eleanore.''

The remaining dregs of bitterness drained away. MacCasky retraced his steps, telling himself he didn't give a damn about the man who'd stolen his mother from him, that he was only doing it for the kid. ''She's about so high—'' He held up a hand. ''Spunky. Doesn't have a whole lot to say for herself, but she eats like a longshoreman, and has more guts than any little girl who looks like a Christmas-tree angel ought to have. I know I was no match for her,'' he added with a reluctant grin.

''Bring her to see me, will you, boy?''

''I may not get the chance. If her mother decides she wants her back, I don't have a leg to stand on.''

''The authorities—''

''Will put her in a foster home.''

''We'll see about that. Tell General Patton that I want my lawyer out here within the hour. You come back this afternoon, boy. I'll have something for you then.''

Mac's hopes, momentarily soaring, plunged again. The old man had skipped the Korean conflict and regressed all the way back to World War Two. "Thanks for your time, sir. If I see General Patton, I'll give him your message."

"Dammit, boy, you'll do as I say! Patton's the one at the front desk—the one with the pig-iron face!"

One look at the name plate that read Genevieve Patton, and Mac was mentally begging the old guy's pardon. He'd been right about her face. The woman looked as if a smile would have fractured her jaw.

A few minutes later he strode through the expensively landscaped grounds to the parking lot, his limp scarcely noticeable. His mind was not on lawyers, or on little girls with large appetites—or even on soft-spoken women whose hair was almost, but not quite, red.

MacCasky had a few ghosts of his own to lay to rest.

One thing Mac had always liked about Conner Jones's modest house in Chesapeake, Virginia, was the furniture. The black leather chairs were big and well broken-in. And the ashtrays. They were the size of dishpans. And the Scotch. It was old enough to vote.

Yet he was still nursing his first drink, and he hadn't smoked a cigarette since he'd got back to the mainland.

"Sure you won't reconsider my offer, Mac?" the older man said.

"Come on, Con—you could lose your job for making an irresponsible move like that. We both know that what I *don't* know about administration would fill the Library of Congress."

"There's a lot to be said for experience."

"There's a lot to be said for retirement."

"I give it two weeks. You'll be weaving pot holders by then."

Mac just grinned. "Maybe I will—maybe I won't. At least grant me the privilege of finding out for myself." If he was going to fall apart, he'd rather do it at a time and place of his own choosing. He had sixty-odd acres out in the middle of nowhere, where he could sit and watch the clouds go by and contemplate his freedom.

"You'll miss it, Mac."

"What, miss having your office on my back to file some report in triplicate? I'll manage somehow."

"The excitement. You've been out there a long time, man—it gets in your blood."

"Yeah, I'm going to miss traveling halfway around the world handcuffed to some lowlife while kids stare at us and whisper and decent folks step back like I was something that would rub off on their clothes. I'm really going to miss crawling on my hands and knees through some stinking swamp, falling flat on my belly every few feet in case a bullet's headed my way."

"It wasn't all bad," Conner reminded him, and Mac knew he was right. There had been good times, good jobs—a lot of satisfaction when it had all worked for him.

Instead of admitting it, he grinned. "Sure. There was the time you sent me out with a pilot who didn't speak English—the guy dropped me on the wrong side of the mountain."

"Hey—mistakes happen." Conner was chuckling now. It hadn't been so funny at the time.

"Yeah, well, next time, try to see that they don't happen while my gut's still in an uproar from eating at the local cantina."

"That kind of thing seldom happens back at the office." Still grinning, Conner finished his drink and reached for the bottle.

"What if I took you up on it? What kind of an agreement could we come to—six-month trial period?"

"On both sides."

"I'll let you know."

Mac stood and looked around for his coat. He'd had no intention of changing his position when he'd come here tonight. The fact that he had was already making him uncomfortable. It had been an instinctive move on his part, and he still wasn't sure what had prompted it. He only knew the answer wasn't here. It was some fifty-odd miles to the south.

"A raccoon!" MacCasky exclaimed later that night. "The hell you say! A *raccoon?*"

"That's what Rosie said. She called not five minutes after you drove off to tell me she knew all about the hole in the roof and the torn screen. They call him Sandy. She says he's as big as a calf and bold as brass, and he's been living there for two years now."

"Cripes! To think I was sneaking around there like James Bond—"

"James Bond never snuck—I've seen all his movies."

"Yeah, well he never got taken in by a damned raccoon, either." Mac knew his face was red. If there was ever a time when a man needed to appear heroic before a woman, this was it. And he didn't. "Look, about the kid," he said, needing to change the subject before he lost his nerve completely. "We've got two things on our side so far—Carol Cargin's note and now this thing from Harrison Keaton."

Watching as Banner examined the notarized statement again, he found himself visually absorbing the texture of her skin, the color of her hair, the pure line of her profile. He'd held the Blazer four-by-four to no more than ten miles above the speed limit, although he'd felt like hiring a chopper. His knee was giving him fits for all the miles he'd driven in the past twenty-four hours. Next time he'd do better to forget his macho image and settle for an automatic drive.

They had adjourned to the living room, and Banner had poured them coffee. Mac was wearing a clean set of jeans and another of the six black flannel shirts he'd bought when he got out of the hospital. He'd borrowed Conner's house for a shower and change of clothes.

Banner, still in the bathrobe and pajamas she'd been wearing when he'd got her out of bed to let him in, laid the papers aside and leveled those molasses-colored eyes at him. "Mac, is there any chance I could adopt her? Would you let me?"

"Sort of transfer ownership, you mean?" At the moment MacCasky had legal guardianship of Tiffany Eleanore Keaton.

"That's one way of putting it, I suppose. But since you're not married—" She looked up then, her face suddenly stricken. "You're not, are you?"

It was all he could do not to reach for her then, but Mac forced himself to take things one step at a time. One *cautious* step at a time. "I'm not married, Banner. I'd never have touched you if I had been. Don't you at least know that much about me by now?"

Wordlessly she nodded.

Mac knew more than enough about her. He knew that he loved her in a way that he had never loved another person in his entire life. He didn't know why, but then he didn't have to know why. It was enough that he knew he loved her.

The trick was in telling her. He'd faced some pretty impossible odds in his life—tackled some projects that had stumped more than one man from more than one agency. T. J. MacCasky, they used to call him—Tough Job MacCasky. He used to go after the hard ones because he liked the challenge. Or maybe it was just because he needed to get his teeth into something and bite down hard.

What he was facing now made those jobs seem like child's play.

He cleared his throat. He considered pouring himself another cup of coffee, but the pot was empty. He cleared his throat again. "Uh...Banner. I'm not a rich man, Banner. I told you I'd turned in my resignation, but—well, we'll get to that in a minute. But even if it doesn't work out, I've saved most of my salary and invested it pretty well. And I've got this farm over in the western part of the state—not that it's much of a place—not very productive, but maybe for a vacation home..."

His voice trailed off as he met her startled look. "MacCasky, what are you trying to say?"

His smile was more nervous than cheerful. "I think I'm offering a testimonial."

"Are you trying to tell me why you'd make a better father than I would a mother?"

He glared at her. "Hell, no! What gave you that idea?"

"Then what are you trying to sell me on, if you don't mind my asking?"

He stood up, stalked across the cluttered room and turned to stare back at her. "Me! What the devil did you think I was selling?"

"I wasn't sure. I'm still not."

He looked at her for a long time, trying to find the words to explain his doubts, his fears—the uncertainty of an unsigned note and a notarized letter written by a prominent Virginia lawyer and countersigned by a probable grandfather. Trying to find the words to tell her how much he loved her and wanted her, no matter what the future brought.

Banner could hardly breathe. He'd come back. He hadn't touched her, but he had hardly taken his eyes off her since she'd let him in the house.

He'd been pale the first time she'd ever seen him. Having learned something of what he'd been through from back issues of the *Daily Advance* that had piled up while she'd been gone, she could understand it.

But he was even paler now. "Mac, just tell me what's wrong. I'll do anything I can to help you. If that means giving up Ellie, then I'll do it, of course. She was never mine. I just want you to be happy, because—" She stopped abruptly. The silence was profound.

"Because?" he prompted.

"Because I love you both too much to do anything else," she admitted, for once making no effort to hide her feelings.

Mac was beside her in an instant. He kicked aside one of the three footstools that cluttered the floor, skirted the coffee table and reached for her hands. "Banner, what did you say?"

"That I love you both too much to—"

"You love me," he said, both his tone and his expression awed. "This isn't just the heat of the moment, is it? You really do love me? Does this mean you're willing to take a chance on me?"

Her hands turned under his until she was clasping his wrists. "It's not the heat of the moment, and I really do mean it, but maybe you'd better explain what you mean by taking a chance."

"Oh, God, she loves me," Mac said softly to the tarnished brass ceiling fixture. And then he was dragging her into his arms, across his lap and pressing kisses on everything he could reach—her cheek, her shoulder, her temple. "Do you have any idea how that makes me feel?"

"I'm not sure. You're awfully good at hiding things."
She laughed a little breathlessly. Turning her face into his
throat, she began kissing, nibbling, inhaling the clean,
masculine scent of his body. "How *does* it make you feel,
MacCasky?"

"What you're doing right now? It makes me want to
take you to bed, woman. But before we do that, let me get
this straight. You said you love me. Does that mean you'd
risk marrying me?"

He could feel the sudden tension in her body. It echoed
the tension in his. "Risk?" she queried. "As in, let's try it
for a few months and see what happens?"

"No, sweetheart, as in let's try it for a lifetime and see
if you can hack it with a guy who doesn't have much to
offer in the way of looks, or job security, or—"

"Does he offer anything besides a wonderful daughter
and an unproductive farm?"

"Does love count?"

He held his breath and waited, afraid of what she was
going to say—afraid he might miss it because his heart was
pounding in his ears. Nothing had ever mattered so much
to him in his life. Curled up in his lap, smelling of citrus,
cinnamon and warm, sexy woman, Banner was all the
good things he'd always wanted but never dared hope for.

"Love counts most of all," she said at last. There were
tears in her voice, as well as her eyes, and damned if he
didn't feel like shedding a few himself.

"You'll have all you ever need of that and then some,
darling. That comes with a lifetime guarantee." And then
he laughed abruptly. "I can't believe I just said that! I'm
the guy who doesn't believe in guarantees. I never believed in tomorrow, or love—I sure as hell wasn't the marrying kind."

"Are you trying to back out already?" she asked calmly.

But Mac was on to her by now. He knew what was hiding under that lovely, calm facade of hers, and he just smiled and lowered her down onto the sofa. Reaching down, he shucked off his boots. One of them fell onto one of her bunny slippers and toppled over. Neither of them noticed it. "Nope. Not now, not tomorrow, not in a million years."

"I'll settle for the next fifty," she said, her eyes brimming with tears and love and laughter.

"Don't try to shortchange me now, sweetheart," he said with a grin as he reached over and snapped off the light. "I'm not sure how we're going to manage your teaching with my marshaling and our parenting, but I've always been pretty good at improvising."

"Aren't we supposed to be farmers, too?"

"Beats me. It'll make a nice place for family vacations. I understand there are several big supermarkets not too far away, and the creek seldom rises more than a few feet."

Mac was lying on top of her, trying to spare her his weight and at the same time loosen her bathrobe, while Banner worked on the buttons of his shirt. "It occurs to me that this is not exactly the way two mature adults are supposed to go about planning the future," she said, her voice brimming with warm laughter.

"Sure it is, sweetheart. It takes two people who've been through some tough times to know how to appreciate the real thing when it comes along." He kissed her nose, and his lips strayed to the corner of her mouth. Lifting them just a fraction, he whispered, "And once you find it, you latch on to it, because something this good doesn't come along more than once in a lifetime."

Banner gave one fleeting thought to the love she had once believed in and lost—to the child who hadn't lived to play with stuffed monkeys or to chase lazy old tomcats under a kitchen table.

Her arms tightened around the man who was holding
er, and she gave herself up to the compelling magic of his
iss.

This was MacCasky, and he was all hers. And their
nce-in-a-lifetime was just now beginning.

Epilogue

Banner watched her last two students drive off befor
turning to go inside. At last! Now she could finish the las
monkey. Removing her paint-stained smock to reveal th
pink one beneath, she hurried to the powder room to was
her hands. Mac and Ellie would be here in less than a
hour. They'd driven out to the nursing home to visit th
Colonel after school today. Usually all three of them wen
on Saturdays, but Ellie had wanted to tell her grandfathe
about the new baby she was going to have. Since his las
stroke, the Colonel couldn't speak, not that that seeme
to hamper his relationship with his granddaughter. Elli
talked enough for both of them, and the old man smile
and sometimes cried a little, and she would let him hol
her monkey until he felt better.

Gaudy, Banner judged some twenty minutes later, ad
miring her handiwork. Eleven monkeys climbed the side
of the towering devil's food cake, some hoisting other

toward the top, a few reaching up onto the top layer toward the Merry-Go-Round of candle holders.

Ellie would love it. She would have a name for every one of the monkeys before the first slice was removed. She had named the mutt they'd adopted from the pound when they'd first moved into the Chesapeake house, the two cats that had adopted *them*, the trees in the big backyard, and even the birds that flocked to the feeder, never mind that Caspar might be a chickadee one day and a blue jay the next.

Hearing a car door slam in the driveway, Banner peered into the mirror and smoothed her hair. She removed the paintbrush she'd forgotten and left rammed through her topknot, and straightened the collar of her maternity smock. Ellie had picked it out, just as she had picked out names for the baby who would be born any day now. Magic Johnson for a boy, Princess Peppertree, after their neighbor's poodle, if it turned out to be a girl.

They were going to have to do some negotiating before too much longer.

"Honey? You all right in there?"

Banner heard the sound of Mac's boots coming down the hall, and she opened the door and walked into his outstretched arms. "I'm all right in there, out here, and especially..." She took his hand and placed it on her swollen middle. "Especially in here."

Mac closed his eyes for a moment and tried to work up a firm enough expression to convince her that she needed to give up teaching until after the baby came. As usual, he got nowhere. All she had to do was look at him with those big, sleepy, molasses-colored eyes of hers, and he fell apart. You would think a man who'd been married nearly two years would be able to do better than that, but there was something about her. Just as there had been something about the sprout, right from the first. Something that cut through every single defensive system he'd built up over a lifetime and homed in on his heart.

Sometimes in the night, he would lie there beside her, after making love—or lately, just holding her hand and aching to make love—and he'd tell himself that it couldn't last. That she'd wake up one day and realize that she had tied herself down to a tired old warhorse with no looks, no charm, and no fortune.

His arms tightened. His mouth moved over the hand she'd lifted to his face, and he drew her fingertips between his teeth. "Hmmm. Turpentine, right?" It was a standing joke between them—that she always smelled of orange peel, cinnamon and turpentine.

"Nope. Chocolate monkeys."

He groaned. "Not another pet!"

"Ellie's birthday cake."

"Honey, don't you think you ought to lie down now? You've been on your feet all day."

"And what position would you recommend?" Banner teased.

Mac's gray eyes glinted as his hands moved down over her newly full breasts. But before he could reply, the back door slammed and a small green-eyed girl with blond pigtails bounced into view.

"Mama, could we name the new baby Colonel after Granddaddy? He told me today he wanted me to."

Mac looked at Banner. Banner looked at Mac. Then Mac bent down, favoring his stiff knee, until he was on a level with his adopted daughter. "Baby, I think that's a fine idea, but Colonel isn't your grandfather's name, it's his rank. Uh, sort of like a title."

Ellie frowned. "Oh. Then could we name him after granddaddy's little boy? His name was Rory, and he used to be my daddy before I got a real one."

Mac took the small, vibrant face between his hard hands, and Banner turned away to hide a sudden burgeoning of tears. "I think that would be a right fine name, sprout. Rory Ford it is, then, if your Mama says it's all right."

"But o' course, if she's a little girl baby," the child said gravely, "we can still name her Princess Peppertree."

After the back door slammed again and Mac was alone with his wife, he braced himself on the door facing and stood. Banner turned to rest her forehead on his shoulder. "Did anyone ever tell you you were a pushover, Mr. Ford?" she asked softly.

"A pushover? *Me?* What the devil ever gave you a crazy notion like that, woman?"

* * * * *

SILHOUETTE® *Desire*™

COMING NEXT MONTH

Take 4 bestselling love stories FREE

Plus get a FREE surprise gift!

Special Limited-time Offer

Mail to
Silhouette Reader Service™
3010 Walden Avenue
P.O. Box 1867
Buffalo, N.Y. 14269-1867

YES! Please send me 4 free Silhouette Desire® novels and my free surprise gift. Then send me 6 brand-new novels every month, which I will receive months before they appear in bookstores. Bill me at the low price of $2.47 each—a savings of 28¢ apiece off cover prices. There are no shipping, handling or other hidden costs. I understand that accepting the books and gift places me under no obligation ever to buy any books. I can always return a shipment and cancel at any time. Even if I never buy another book from Silhouette, the 4 free books and the surprise gift are mine to keep forever.

225 BPA AC7P

Name _____ (PLEASE PRINT)

Address _____ Apt. No. _____

City _____ State _____ Zip _____

This offer is limited to one order per household and not valid to present Silhouette Desire® subscribers. Terms and prices are subject to change. Sales tax applicable in N.Y.

DES-BPA2DR

© 1990 Harlequin Enterprises Limited

WIN
CARS,TRIPS,CASH!

SILHOUETTE®
OFFICIAL SWEEPSTAKES
RULES

NO PURCHASE NECESSARY

1. To enter, complete an Official Entry Form or 3" × 5" index card by hand-printing, in plain block letters, your complete name, address, phone number and age, and mailing it to: Silhouette Fashion A Whole New You Sweepstakes, P.O. Box 9056, Buffalo, NY 14269-9056.

   No responsibility is assumed for lost, late or misdirected mail. Entries must be sent separately with first class postage affixed, and be received no later than December 31, 1991 for eligibility.

2. Winners will be selected by D.L. Blair, Inc., an independent judging organization whose decisions are final, in random drawings to be held on January 30, 1992 in Blair, NE at 10:00 a.m. from among all eligible entries received.

3. The prizes to be awarded and their approximate retail values are as follows: Grand Prize — A brand-new Ford Explorer 4×4 plus a trip for two (2) to Hawaii, including round-trip air transportation, six (6) nights hotel accommodation, a $1400 meal/spending money stipend and $2,000 cash toward a new fashion wardrobe (approximate value: $28,000) or $15,000 cash; two (2) Second Prizes — A trip to Hawaii, including round-trip air transportation, six (6) nights hotel accommodation, a $1,400 meal/spending money stipend and $2,000 cash toward a new fashion wardrobe (approximate value: $11,000) or $5,000 cash; three (3) Third Prizes — $2,000 cash toward a new fashion wardrobe. All prizes are valued in U.S. currency. Travel award air transportation is from the commercial airport nearest winner's home. Travel is subject to space and accommodation availability, and must be completed by June 30, 1993. Sweepstakes offer is open to residents of the U.S. and Canada who are 21 years of age or older as of December 31, 1991, except residents of Puerto Rico, employees and immediate family members of Torstar Corp., its affiliates, subsidiaries, and all agencies, entities and persons connected with the use, marketing, or conduct of this sweepstakes. All federal, state, provincial, municipal and local laws apply. Offer void wherever prohibited by law. Taxes and/or duties, applicable registration and licensing fees, are the sole responsibility of the winners. Any litigation within the province of Quebec respecting the conduct and awarding of a prize may be submitted to the Régie des loteries et courses du Québec. All prizes will be awarded; winners will be notified by mail. No substitution of prizes is permitted.

4. Potential winners must sign and return any required Affidavit of Eligibility/Release of Liability within 30 days of notification. In the event of noncompliance within this time period, the prize may be awarded to an alternate winner. Any prize or prize notification returned as undeliverable may result in the awarding of that prize to an alternate winner. By acceptance of their prize, winners consent to use of their names, photographs or their likenesses for purposes of advertising, trade and promotion on behalf of Torstar Corp. without further compensation. Canadian winners must correctly answer a time-limited arithmetical question in order to be awarded a prize.

5. For a list of winners (available after 3/31/92), send a separate stamped, self-addressed envelope to: Silhouette Fashion A Whole New You Sweepstakes, P.O. Box 4665, Blair, NE 68009.

PREMIUM OFFER TERMS

To receive your gift, complete the Offer Certificate according to directions. Be certain to enclose the required number of "Fashion A Whole New You" proofs of product purchase (which are found on the last page of every specially marked "Fashion A Whole New You" Silhouette or Harlequin romance novel). Requests must be received no later than December 31, 1991. Limit: four (4) gifts per name, family, group, organization or address. Items depicted are for illustrative purposes only and may not be exactly as shown. Please allow 6 to 8 weeks for receipt of order. Offer good while quantities of gifts last. In the event an ordered gift is no longer available, you will receive a free, previously unpublished Silhouette or Harlequin book for every proof of purchase you have submitted with your request, plus a refund of the postage and handling charge you have included. Offer good in the U.S. and Canada only.

SLFW-SWPR

SILHOUETTE® OFFICIAL SWEEPSTAKES ENTRY FORM

4-FWSDS-4

Complete and return this Entry Form immediately – the more entries you submit, the better your chances of winning!

- Entries must be received by December 31, 1991.
- A Random draw will take place on January 30, 1992.
- No purchase necessary.

Yes, I want to win a FASHION A WHOLE NEW YOU Sensuous and Adventurous prize from Silhouette:

Name _____ Telephone _____ Age _____

Address _____

City _____ State _____ Zip _____

Return Entries to: Silhouette **FASHION A WHOLE NEW YOU**,
P.O. Box 9056, Buffalo, NY 14269-9056   © 1991 Harlequin Enterprises Limited

PREMIUM OFFER

To receive your free gift, send us the required number of proofs-of-purchase from any specially marked FASHION A WHOLE NEW YOU Silhouette or Harlequin Book with the Offer Certificate properly completed, plus a check or money order (do not send cash) to cover postage and handling payable to Silhouette FASHION A WHOLE NEW YOU Offer. We will send you the specified gift.

OFFER CERTIFICATE

Item	A. SENSUAL DESIGNER VANITY BOX COLLECTION (set of 4) (Suggested Retail Price $60.00)	B. ADVENTUROUS TRAVEL COSMETIC CASE SET (set of 3) (Suggested Retail Price $25.00)
# of proofs-of-purchase	18	12
Postage and Handling	$3.50	$2.95
Check one	☐	☐

Name _____

Address _____

City _____ State _____ Zip _____

Mail this certificate, designated number of proofs-of-purchase and check or money order for postage and handling to: Silhouette **FASHION A WHOLE NEW YOU** Gift Offer, P.O. Box 9057, Buffalo, NY 14269-9057. Requests must be received by December 31, 1991.

ONE PROOF-OF-PURCHASE

4-FWSDP-4

To collect your fabulous free gift you must include the necessary number of proofs-of-purchase with a properly completed Offer Certificate.

© 1991 Harlequin Enterprises Limited

See previous page for details.